SEDGE-HILL SETTER

SEDGE-HILL SETTER

BY

Tom Person

ILLUSTRATED BY HARPER JOHNSON

LONGMANS, GREEN AND CO.

NEW YORK · LONDON · TORONTO

LONGMANS, GREEN AND CO., INC.
119 WEST 40TH STREET, NEW YORK 18

LONGMANS, GREEN AND CO., LTD.
6 & 7 CLIFFORD STREET, LONDON W 1

LONGMANS, GREEN AND CO.
20 CRANFIELD ROAD, TORONTO 16

SEDGE-HILL SETTER

PUBLISHED SIMULTANEOUSLY IN THE DOMINION OF CANADA BY
LONGMANS, GREEN AND CO., TORONTO

To
CURTIS PERSON

*May his black-and-white "Old Sport"
find countless coveys in Elysian fields.*

SEDGE-HILL SETTER

1

IF YOU GO EAST OF MEMPHIS, AND SOUTH A LITTLE, YOU WILL come to sedge-hill country. Not far beyond the edge of it, where pines begin to rear dark against the waist-high tan sedge, you will enter what was once the quail-hunting paradise of the Tomlins. Old men with good memories can look back in their minds and see on each hill and in each hollow a big Llewellyn setter flowing tirelessly, head high, broad black ears flopping; or perhaps they can see just as vividly such a magnificent black-and-white setter frozen to marble on point. It was Tomlin country for three generations, and some Tomlin dog must in that time have covered every square foot of the extensive domain.

It was a soft-aired April morning, with dogwoods flashing white against the new green of woods that rimmed the winding road, when Lee Langston and his father drove to the Tomlin place. In one mile they flushed three pairs of quail from the weedy roadside and watched them fly, low and level, into nearby thickets of plum, sumac or pine.

"Looks like a fine crop of birds coming on," Mr. Langston said as the third pair of brown birds sailed into their chosen covert.

"You see more of 'em now than when the season opens,"

Lee pointed out. "Each pair we see in spring ought to have its own covey in the fall. What becomes of them?"

The man pointed toward the pale horizon. "Yonder's one reason for fewer coveys than there are paired-off birds."

Lee looked that way. A hawk almost the size of a turkey buzzard was wheeling above the trees in the distance, circling slowly in search of unwary prey.

Mr. Langston went on, "Stray cats, egg-eating dogs, foxes—"

"I'd like to take a pop at that hawk!" the boy broke in, his blue eyes alight. "Will I have a gun this fall, you reckon?"

"I hunted with one before I was fourteen," his father answered slowly. Then, after a pause that Lee knew the reason for, he added, "Your mama's mortally afraid of guns. You know that."

They rode on in silence, save for the rattle of the pickup truck, which Lee and his father used in their going and coming, for they left the car for Mrs. Langston's use. This gun matter had come up before. Lee would be fourteen in the fall, well before the opening of the bird season . . . never called "quail" season in this part of the South. Maybe if Uncle Joe, his mother's brother, hadn't lost an eye while bird hunting she wouldn't be so nervous about guns.

"She ought not to mind a .410," Lee said, breaking the silence.

"It's not the size of the gun that matters so much," the man said. "It's just *gun*." He shrugged almost imperceptibly. "It's been like that a long time."

They came in sight of the old Tomlin house, which had been built years ago of hand-hewn logs. A wide veranda fronted the structure. Leading back from the center of the veranda was the breezeway, or "dog-trot," which ran the full depth of the building. Four rooms opened onto the breezeway. The house stood on a slight rise in a scattering of tall, wide-armed white oaks.

As the Langston truck pulled up at the gate in the split-paling fence, old Luke Tomlin came onto the porch. He was tall, gaunt and straight, with a shock of white hair that had once been red.

"Get out an' come in," he called. "That you, Hurd?"

"Yes, sir." Mr. Langston slid from beneath the wheel. "Where's ol' Saddle? He always meets me here with fight in his eye."

They had gone along the mossy, snaggled brick walk between two thick-matted rows of violets, almost to the steps, before the old man answered. "Saddle died. I buried him yestiddy."

"That so? Well, I'm mighty sorry to hear—"

"Needn't be," the old man cut in. "Saddle was past twelve. Come up an' take rockers. Lee, you're growin' fast."

Lee nodded. He had always viewed old man Tomlin with awe. There was something about the bushy white hair, the craggy face, and the fierce eyebrows sheltering piercing blue eyes, that gave the boy a feeling of littleness. Lee had often wondered if Mr. Tomlin had ever been a young man. He had looked just the same all of Lee's lifetime.

They sat in cane-bottomed rockers that creaked petulantly. Mr. Tomlin was saying, "A fine dog, but I wasn't able to hunt Saddle much. He was a kind of wasted dog, you might say." Then he stopped for a moment, looked out past the white oaks to the rolling sedge hills and hollows. "Hurd, there are few men in the world who are here to do one thing an' know what it is. Mostly they don't know why they're here, so they rattle aroun' like a pea in a bucket. But a Llewellyn setter of the Tomlin strain knew why he was on the good Lord's earth. He was born to find birds!"

"Old Saddle knew that," Mr. Langston said appreciatively. "All the Tomlin dogs have known it. No finer setters ever ran these hills."

Old man Tomlin had leaned back against a veranda post after his dissertation on men and dogs. He nodded slowly. "Your pa an' I used to roam this country back when there *was* birds—your gran'pa, Lee, I'm talkin' about. Why, 'twas nothin' to find thirty coveys in a half-day's hunt. Sometimes we'd take a hundred shells apiece, an' our hosses, an' we'd bring in, sometimes, a hundred an' fifty birds at sundown, with shells left. No limits then, you know." He leaned forward again, the chair complaining. "We was both crack shots—an' young. You've got to be young to do such things, an' not wore out. Saddle was wore out, so he died."

"Pa had a Tomlin dog when I was about Lee's age," Mr. Langston said. "We covered this country together, and I brought home many a good skillet meal."

"The dog you hunted back then was named Buckalew," Mr. Tomlin said, squinting as an aid to memory. "His mama's name was Sallie Ghost, an' his daddy was Ramblin' Sam."

"Right!" Mr. Langston exclaimed. "You've a real memory for dogs."

"Things back then are clearer than what happened yestiddy," the old man declared. "An' another thing, back then we lived an' breathed dogs. That line of setters, which my pa developed, was the most important thing on earth to us. There was no closed season, no restrictions, an' we shot up the birds pretty bad, I reckin." He sighed. "It was good times an' prosperity—a day that'll never come back. An' if it did," he added slowly, his eyes roaming again to the hills and hollows, "I'd be too wore out to do anything about it."

"We have more birds hereabouts than in most places," Mr. Langston said. "And that brings me around to why I came out this morning. There's a man named Winston, from Memphis, who's feeling out the landowners around here about selling him hunting rights. He figures to bring in city folks and charge them big prices to stay at the fine hotel he plans to build. He'll furnish guides and dogs—"

"I heard about the fellow," Mr. Tomlin interrupted. A hard light shone in the old man's eyes. "Better keep him out. It'd be the end of huntin' for the home folks here if he came in an' started such a business."

"That's how Jim Webb and I feel about it," Mr. Langston said. "We want to keep this country as near like it was when we grew up, so our boys can enjoy it, too."

"But the big landowners are the ones to be convinced," Mr. Tomlin said. "What they'd get for huntin' rights would be like gravy. Take Joe Ray, now; he don't hunt, an' he don't care who does or don't. All he wants is the almighty dollar."

"Webb and I are going to see him and Jim Andrews before long," Mr. Langston said. "Maybe we can talk them out of selling hunting rights."

"You'll have to talk fast," Mr. Tomlin said grimly. "A dollar has a mighty slick tongue." Then he left his rocker, saying, "Come on, Lee. I want to show you a pup out there in the kennel."

Lee's heart beat fast. Something in the old man's tone and manner had excited him. He got up, beckoning his dad to follow.

There were four wobbly, black-and-white puppies in the

pen. The rangy mother barked at the strangers, but more in recognition of them than in anger. The little ones, about six weeks old, ran to the wire, tumbling over each other, and reared up on it, yipping and whining. They were roly-poly, knobby-legged, with broad ears and stubby muzzles. All were black-and-white. One was smaller than the other three.

Mr. Tomlin leaned over the fence, talked gently to them. Then he reached through the wire and roughed them up playfully before scooping up the smaller one and bringing it through the opening between the mesh wire and the strand of barbed wire just above it.

"This one's the runt," he said softly, stroking its black ears. "It's the only male of the lot, an' his greedy sisters are eatin' him out of growth an' comfort!"

"Let me hold him," Lee asked, reaching for the little fellow.

"Sure." Old man Tomlin relinquished the pup. "He looks a lot like ol' Saddle. See? Black across the back, an' black all over one side of his face." And after a pause, "This is the last male dog of the Tomlin line."

Lee held the pup, felt its excited heart beating swiftly. Then he dodged with poor success as the pup's eager red tongue swiped at his chin.

"He likes you," Mr. Langston said, amused.

"It's the nature of these dogs to be friendly," Mr. Tomlin said. "They like anybody who'll show them some kindness an' interest." He leaned against the fence, looking out over the hollow and to the woods beyond. Obviously he was thinking hard about something, for his bushy brows were working. He turned slowly back to Lee.

"You remind me a little of your gran'pa, boy. I was thinkin' . . . " His voice trailed off. He was looking at Lee, but it

"I'll be good to him," Lee promised happily

was plain that his mind was more occupied with another time, another place.

The puppy whined and squirmed, happy over such unaccustomed attention. The mother dog reared up on the fence and barked loudly for the return of her little one.

Mr. Tomlin returned to reality. His mouth was set hard. "They all went off an' left me," he said abruptly. "This, out here in the sticks, wasn't good enough for them." He stopped there and cleared his throat. His busy brows contracted into a frown. "You can have the pup, son."

Lee almost dropped the little fellow. "I—can—have—?"

"Well, now, Mr. Tomlin—" Mr. Langston began.

"You had the gran'daddy of this pup about ten 'great-greats' ago," the old man cut in. "It's time your boy had a Tomlin dog . . . an' this is the last chance he'll ever have. I'm shippin' the other three pups an' their mammy to a man in Chicago 'fore long."

"It's mighty nice of you to do this for Lee," Mr. Langston put in.

"Forget it," Mr. Tomlin said gruffly. "There's more to it than just the dog business."

"I'll be good to him," Lee promised happily. "I'll fatten him up, and he'll grow to a big dog. I'll—"

"There are two things about Tomlin setters," the old man broke in. "They've got the best noses in this country, an' they're hardheaded with spirit." He laughed shortly. "Maybe they take after the Tomlins!"

On the way home Lee held the pup and hoped to high heaven it escaped being carsick. "What do you s'pose Mama'll say?" he wondered aloud.

"We may have to talk pretty fast." Mr. Langston spoke

gently, but there was a look in his eyes. "Your mama's people, except for your uncle Joe, never fished or hunted much, and Joe never hunted after getting that stray shot in his eye."

Lee said nothing for a while. "What did Mr. Tomlin mean," he asked finally, "when he said there was more to it than just the dog business?"

"Well, the old fellow has been hurt pretty deep, son. Both his boys went off to town when they were grown. Guy Tomlin was really an adopted son. They could've carried on the training business, for he'd taught them well, but they didn't care about slow country life."

"Will Tomlin was killed in the war, wasn't he?"

"That's right. It was a terrible blow. Then Will's widow remarried, and old Mr. and Mrs. Tomlin took Mary Lou, Will's daughter, to raise. She was a great comfort to the old man, especially after his wife passed away. Sort of made up for the other disappointments."

"Then Mary Lou up an' married," Lee added.

His father nodded. "It was a tough disappointment when she ran off with Embry Wales. The Tomlins and the Waleses, who were sort of second-rate dog trainers, never did get along well, anyhow. I guess Embry was a little wild, too. Mr. Tomlin won't have anything to do with him."

Mrs. Langston was in the kitchen, finishing with dinner, when they reached home. Lee and his dad went in together, both braced for the protests they were sure would come.

"You're just in time." Then she turned and saw Lee with the pup cradled in his arms. Her blue eyes widened, and she stiffened perceptibly. "Oh, my goodness!" she exclaimed, dismay showing through. "Where did you pick up that poor little thing?"

"Mr. Tomlin gave it to me." Lee was pleased with the hint of sympathy she had given. "It's the runt of the litter."

"It must be!" she said with a quick glance at her husband. It was plain that this was a moment she had foreseen with vague dread. She turned back to Lee. "It's one of those Tomlins, I guess."

"Yes, it's the last son dog of old Saddle," Mr. Langston told her. "He died yesterday."

She turned back to the wood range and took a skillet of brown-crusted cornbread from the oven. "Saddle was right old." And without looking at Lee she said, "Go put the puppy in that big box on the back porch, and wash up for dinner."

Fully aware that she had said "the puppy" instead of "your puppy" and that this carried a strong hint of refusal, Lee went out. From the back porch he caught her words, "Doesn't need a bird dog." That was it, of course: "*bird dog.*" That kind of dog meant a gun and shooting. She might not object to just a dog, but she was frightened by what a bird dog stood for.

Nothing was said of the pup during the noon meal. Mr. Langston reported on the trip to the Tomlin place, and they felt sorry for the old man, so alone now. It was a shame that Mary Lou and Embry, struggling along in Memphis on a factory job, couldn't make up with Mr. Tomlin and come to live with him. Embry wasn't at all lazy, and he had turned out to be steady and dependable. It would help Mr. Tomlin to have young people near him, particularly Mary Lou.

"He fairly worships her," Mrs. Langston declared, "but just because she married a Wales, he disowns her. How hardheaded can a man be!"

"If the old fellow ever came down sick, he'd really need Mary Lou," Mr. Langston said. "He couldn't turn to Guy for help, and that's for sure."

The pup was being stubbornly ignored. It was a matter that had to be dealt with, but Mr. and Mrs. Langston were carefully postponing it. Considering the noises that were arising from the box on the back porch, this was something of an accomplishment, for the puppy was whining almost steadily. He broke the monotony of this by yipping occasionally in a high, sharp voice. As an accompaniment to these vocal exercises, he was almost continuously scratching on the sides of the box, trying to climb out. Now and then he fell back with a soft, scrambling thump, only to get up again and resume his objections to the shameful imprisonment that had befallen him.

"He's a stubborn little cuss!" At last Mr. Langston pushed back his chair. "Give him a saucer of milk, Lee. Boys and puppies are usually starved."

The diagnosis proved good. Lee sat on the edge of the porch and laughed at the runt's clumsiness in dealing with the milk. In seconds, his broad muzzle was whitewashed, even up to the eye on the black side of his face. The messy discoloration gave him an even more rakish leer as he peered up at his new master and wagged his stubby tail. Then he stepped on the edge of the saucer and spilled the rest of the milk, which he promptly tried to lap up from the seasoned boards on which it ran in every direction.

The question of a name arose that evening. "It ought to be somethin' that'll hook him up with ol' Saddle," Lee reasoned. "And different enough to make it his own name at the same time."

"You've been thinking about it all afternoon, I'll bound you!" his mother accused.

"The pup won't hurt his work," Mr. Langston said. And, to Lee, "He has a saddle, too. I believe it'll be wider and more solid than old Saddle's was."

"How 'bout 'Black Saddle'?" Lee asked. "It'll describe him an' be like his daddy's name, yet different, too."

"It fits him, all right," Mrs. Langston agreed. "Black covers his back like a saddle, and it's as dark as a moonless night."

" 'Black Saddle' will be a long name," Mr. Langston predicted. "We won't call him that."

"It'll turn out 'Blackie,' " said Mrs. Langston, "or maybe just 'Saddle,' or even 'Sad.' "

" 'Sad' won't fit him right," Lee declared. "He'll be a happy-natured, slap-happy dog. You watch."

"What about 'Clown'?" Mr. Langston offered. "The way his little face is marked, that would fit him pretty well."

But Lee held out for "Black Saddle," and they agreed to call him that until some appropriate name came out of it.

Of course, as things happened, it mattered little what he was called, for he would be the same dog, hardheaded with spirit and blessed with the gifts of his kind.

"Old Saddle," Mr. Langston recalled, "was an all-round dog. You could take him out hunting at night, and he'd tree 'possums. You could go out when the snow was on the ground, and he'd hunt rabbits, burrowing into the drifts and bringing 'em out alive, scarcely marked. But on a good day for birds, Saddle would hunt quail and never even sniff at a cottontail. That dog had man-sense, almost!"

"How was he at retrievin'?" Lee inquired.

"Tops. When a bird crumpled up in the air, at the crack of

a gun, Saddle had him nearly as soon as he hit the ground. Crippled birds never got away from him. He'd get 'em out of sinkholes, hollow logs—no matter where."

"Your puppy will be just a pet, though," Mrs. Langston said firmly. "He won't be a hunting dog."

Lee and his father were very quiet. Here it was, out in the open at last! Here was the thing that Lee had awaited and feared. His mother was, even this early, offsetting any plans of his that might require a gun.

"Let time decide that," Mr. Langston said gently. "We're crossing the bridge before—"

"But I can see what's coming," she said, her voice a trifle shrill. It was evident that much feeling and keen dread had dammed up and were now overflowing with her words.

"Lee will grow bigger," Mr. Langston pointed out, speaking calmly. "The puppy will grow up fast and, unless we settle this thing now, it'll always be something we've got to face—"

"You know how I feel about guns," she interrupted. "Lee will not be a bird hunter!"

"You said Black Saddle wouldn't be a hunting dog, and now you say Lee won't be a bird hunter."

"Well, it's all the same thing," she said sharply. "If one hunts, the other will, too. I'm trying to get my say in before it's too late."

By now the whining and wailing of the puppy in the box was so loud and insistent that something had to be done. Lee went out onto the back porch and picked him up, talking softly and petting him. The little fellow was lonely. This was his first time away from his mother and his littermates. Lee brought out another saucer of milk and fed the pup, talking quietly to him, saying, "Sh-wuh! Sh-wuh!"

It was not a good night at the Langston house. Black Saddle filled it with noises and protesting. The only relief came after Lee had sated him with milk, and this was brief respite from the whines and yips. It was nothing short of a miracle that the skinny little fellow, ballooned and paunchy from overfeeding, had the stamina to keep up his whining and yelping. But he did.

"Hardheaded with spirit," old Mr. Tomlin had said, Lee recalled. Well, whatever the pup was hardheaded with, he had plenty of it!

Lee tumbled and tossed in his bed upstairs. Now and then another breath, Lee could hear his mother and father talking. during the night's brief silences, when the pup was taking There was, he was sure, a definite edge to his mother's voice.

Deep in the night, miserable over the increasingly difficult position he held as the master of Black Saddle, Lee slipped from bed and went downstairs to the back porch. When he gathered up the puppy, it snuggled close and slurped its hot, wet tongue across his cheek. He whispered to it, stroked its soft ears, reassured it, aware that at the very second these attentions ceased, the noises would resume.

He heard footsteps within the house. The back screen door opened, and his mother said quietly, "Go back to bed, Lee. You can't spend the night like this. You'll spoil him worse, and we'll have a harder time than ever."

"Yes'm." Lee put the little fellow back into the box and left him there. He was barely back in the house when the puppy raised its keen voice to new heights of protest.

At breakfast Mrs. Langston said wearily, "Now, that was a night! Another one like it, and we'll all be candidates for the asylum! That includes the pup, too!"

"He won't be that bad again," Lee promised, desperately hoping there was some basis for his optimism. "The first night's the worst. You watch."

"Maybe you'd better put him out in the barn tonight when he starts his foolishness," his mother suggested.

"Aw, now, Nell," Mr. Langston objected. "It wasn't that bad." He controlled a yawn. "Right pitiful how lonesome he was, I thought."

"You're both against me!" she scolded, setting hot biscuits on the table. Then, as if inspired, "Lee, I've thought of something. If your dog *has* to be hunted, let Mr. Webb train and hunt him. He's good with bird dogs, isn't he?"

"He's rough on dogs," Lee told her. "I saw him whip a pointer with a hick'ry shoot one day last winter, just because the dog had flushed a single. I thought he'd kill the poor thing."

"Bird dogs are hardheaded," Mr. Langston said. "Jim Webb knows how to handle 'em. He's always got good dogs."

"No use to half kill a dog because he flushes a bird," Lee declared.

"I've seen hunters shoot pretty good dogs just for flushing," Mr. Langston told him. "It's surprising how a dog'll settle down and be careful after being burnt with a load of light shot."

"You never saw Mr. Tomlin shoot a dog, did you?" Lee asked.

"Never hunted much with him." Mr. Langston took time buttering a biscuit. "Takes rough punishment to convince a dog, sometimes."

Lee gave the matter thought. Raising and training a bird dog appeared to have a variety of difficult angles.

ᏗᎦ 2 ᎦᎢ

WHILE HIS FATHER ATTENDED A MEETING OF THE LANDOWNERS that evening, Lee built a doghouse. To save having to repeat the job later, he made it big enough for a grown dog.

"He'll never be *that* big," Mrs. Langston said. "Aren't you afraid he'll get lost in there and starve before he finds his way out again?"

Lee grinned. "It's big, all right, but in a few months Black Saddle will be big enough for it. Look at his ears and feet, he'll be a whopper."

When he had finished with the doghouse, Lee dragged it to the back porch and started shoving it under, as a precaution against leaks in case he had done a poor job of roofing.

"Not there," his mother objected. "If that pup has fleas, we'll have them all over the house."

Lee hauled it out and placed it under the chinaberry tree in the middle of the back yard. He would of course keep Black Saddle completely flealess, but there was no future in arguing with his mother about that.

Lee's heart beat fast when he thought of the pup as a grown dog, legs and tail feathered out. He could see the rangy fellow coursing the sedge hills and valleys in search of birds— now he was trotting high-headed along a ridge, "winding"

16

birds, straining from the vagrant breeze the marvelous odor of quail—now frozen on point, right forefoot off the ground, folded back lightly. In the fleeting vision he saw Black Saddle's pointing form clearly: head and back making a level line, tail continuing it, but curving slightly upward toward the tip.

And Lee Langston's vision extended: He saw himself with a brand-new gun, a sixteen- or a twenty-gauge, coming up behind the still setter, and he could fairly hear himself saying, "Whoa, Black Saddle—easy, Sad!" Then he would walk in ahead of the dog and flush the birds. They would burst in a roaring explosion from the clump of sedge just ahead of Sad, and Lee's gun would crack twice, neatly dropping two limp quail into the grass . . .

There was no end to the dream. It went on and on: coveys, singles, maybe an occasional cripple, with Black Saddle always true on point, sure and graceful in retrieving. The last Tomlin, once a runt, was now big and beautiful as a calendar dog, ever the hero, the perfect performer. Some day, perhaps, Black Saddle would be good enough to enter field trials, maybe even the Great Southern—

"Lord, that's really dreamin'!" Lee said hoarsely.

He took the pup from the big box on the back porch and shoved him into the new doghouse. "Go to bed," he ordered gently. But when he reached to shut the door, he found it very hard to seal the lonely little fellow off from the world. So he left the door almost closed, giving Black Saddle a choice.

When Lee straightened up and turned away, the pup made its choice without delay. With a desperate yip he piled out of the door, and loped, falling twice, in pursuit of his master. They gained the back steps at exactly the same second.

"Clumsy, isn't he?" Mrs. Langston said from just inside the

back door, from which point she had been watching. "Is he crippled?"

"He's just six weeks old," Lee reminded her. "You wait; he'll be as stout as a mule before long."

"I'll wait," she promised. "That's about all I can do, with both you and your daddy so thoroughly sold on the measly little thing. For goodness' sake, don't let him get under the house! He could howl all night, and we'd never be able to get to him."

"Yes'm, I won't. But I could call him out. He comes to me. Look." Lee knelt and clapped his hands, saying, "Sh-wuh! here, fella. Come here."

Black Saddle galloped awkwardly toward the boy. He was thrashing his stubby tail and yipping joyously over the game, which was vastly better than imprisonment.

"It worked that time," Mrs. Langston granted, "but if he got scared or excited there under the house, he might not come to you. Shut him in the doghouse tonight."

"It'll make him hate it," Lee told her. "Can't I just put him back in the box tonight, 'til he's more used to bein' in a strange place?"

"Oh, all right," she relented. "But if he carries on like last night, you'll have to do something about it."

"Yes'm." So Lee fed Black Saddle again, making sure the pup was filled to capacity. This should put him to sleep, at least for a while.

Mr. Langston returned from town after Lee had gone upstairs to bed. Lee called down to learn what had happened at the meeting.

"Well, we wrangled a lot," his father reported. "Ray and Jim Andrews still want this Winston to come in here, and they're ready to sell him hunting rights for five years. Did you get the doghouse finished?"

"Yes, sir." And, after a pause, "But he'll be in the box again tonight. He'll be quiet, though; he's so full now he'd howl if he tried to take a deep breath."

"Well, keep him like that," Mr. Langston begged with a chuckle. "We could use a night's sleep."

In spite of Lee's promises and efforts, that night was little better than the one before. There were few short periods of relief. Within two hours the pup began protesting again, whining and clawing at the box and thudding around in it. Lee got up groggily from a deep sleep and stumbled down to the refrigerator for milk.

Black Saddle lapped it up avidly, save for the portion he managed to spill by stepping on the edge of the saucer. Then he flopped down on his sticky, wet bed and returned to his brief coma.

Three times, later in the night, the same routine was repeated. Not long before daybreak Mrs. Langston implored shrilly, "Put him in the doghouse and then shut the door this time." Adding, with a groan, "I'd rather raise triplets!"

It was well after sunrise before the Langstons were up and about.

"The worst is over, I think," Mr. Langston said, forcing optimism.

"If it isn't, I'll soon be over and done with!" Mrs. Langston said miserably. "I feel as if I've been dragged through a knothole backwards. This black coffee looks about the way I feel this morning."

These were not the worst experiences the Langstons had with Black Saddle, but they were representative samples. As the puppy grew in size and experience, he devised new torments. His vocal powers increased, and his whining and yipping grew into prolonged sessions of barking. Moonlight nights seemed to inspire him, and he sat for hours beside his house—the summer nights were too hot for shutting the door on him—and barked almost steadily at nothing at all.

It was Lee's theory that Black Saddle was answering other dogs too distant for human ears to hear, but he could not prove this.

"I hope that's true," Mrs. Langston said one night. "If it isn't, your pup is either downright cruel or crazy!"

"All puppies bark a lot," Mr. Langston reminded her. "Bird dogs are about the worst, I reckon."

"I used to enjoy listening to katydids and whippoorwills," Mrs. Langston said wearily. "Now I do well to hear a big transport truck roar along the highway!"

Mr. Langston knocked out his pipe, sending a spray of fading sparks beyond the edge of the porch. "Go back there, Lee, and take a switch to that pup. He's got to stop barking."

Lee went around to the back yard, but it is not a matter of record that he selected much of a switch or that he wielded it with much authority. Black Saddle protested his punishment with light yelps, then with even more vigor resumed his relentless barking.

"If there's any switching to be done," Mrs. Langston pointed out, "you'll have to do it."

"It's Lee's pet," Mr. Langston reminded her. "He's got to learn to make the pup mind."

"You're just as tender-hearted as Lee," she said with understanding. "Let's go to bed and sleep this one out—if we can get to sleep."

Midnight came before sleep did. Mr. Langston, thoroughly aroused and reckless with misery, left his bed and went outside. He caught up an old scrub broom from its place on the back porch and hurled it without warning at the noisy blur beneath the chinaberry. The whiz of the missile was lost in a wild "YOW-*urp!!*" which merged into a hysteria of barking: "*Bow-wow-wow-wow! Roo! Roo! ROOO-ooooo!*" Then, silence.

Lee ran lightly to his upstairs window, looked out, amazed by his father's wild desperation. He heard the whiz of the broom and its clatter against the doghouse; then he saw the white streak as Black Saddle, bellowing with each leap, shot for the back porch and disappeared beneath it.

"Thank goodness!" Mrs. Langston moaned. "Maybe that's how to make him shut up!"

Her words were scarcely spoken when noise came again from Black Saddle. It was louder now and far more impassioned. In addition to whatever the original purpose of the barking had been, it now carried scolding reproach of the one who had sought to do him harm. He was expressing himself at a point far up under the house. Specifically, he had retired to a point directly beneath the bedroom of Mr. and Mrs. Langston.

Lee was wretched. How long his mother, who had for some time no doubt admired her own patience and forbearance, could endure such torture, he had no way of knowing. But he was convinced of one thing: Black Saddle was fast deteriorating in her estimation.

Deeper in the night, after Mr. and Mrs. Langston had wearily moved to the bedroom at the other end of the house, Black Saddle quieted down for a time. It was during this happy period that he must have abandoned the dark place under the house and returned to the moonlit back yard, for that was where he was located when the earliest roosters crowed to announce the approach of dawn. This shift in operation placed him nearer to the refuge Mr. and Mrs. Langston had selected, and it encouraged them to get up much earlier that morning.

Not long after breakfast, which proved a rather grim meal, Lee went to see Mr. Webb about the matter.

"Barks a lot, does he?" the stocky farmer inquired with poorly veiled amusement.

"And he's worse on moonlight nights," Lee said, swallowing a yawn. "He was awful last night."

"Well, I don't know much you can do about it," the man said. "He sounds about average. A fellow earns any setter pup he raises!"

"But isn't there some way to stop him?" Lee begged.

Mr. Webb scratched his chin slowly. "Yes, you might try a tight muzzle. That might slow him down a little. 'Course it'll make pantin' hard, an' dogs need to pant when they're hot."

"I'd hate to do that to him," Lee said. And, seeking a good reason for not using the tight muzzle, he added, "That'd take all his protection away from him in case he needed to fight back at somethin' in the night."

"Your yard's tight, ain't it?" the farmer asked. "Other dogs won't be gettin' in where he is."

"But a stray cat might jump him some night. Ol' Buster, our tomcat, doesn't like the little fellow, but he's too smart to jump him."

"I can't think of any other way," Mr. Webb said, "unless you have his vocal cords operated on, an' you won't . . ."

"No, sir, not that," Lee broke in. "When he grows up a little more, and gets away from bein' a pup, won't he stop it, maybe?"

Mr. Webb laughed shortly. "I've got a black-an'-white setter that's eight year old, an' he still barks a lot at night." He looked at Lee for a moment. "I'll be glad to take 'im off your hands. Will you take five dollars for him?"

"Black Saddle's not for sale," Lee replied firmly. "I'm goin' to raise him. Besides, he was given to me."

"Well, I didn't figure you'd sell the pup—but keep me in mind if you ever decided to get rid of him. I like them Tomlin dogs."

The problem of Black Saddle's nightly serenades remained. A disturbing feature of the matter was that his voice grew in quality and carrying power in proportion to his growth in stature. Another increase was obvious, too, and that was his ability to bark longer at a stretch without pausing for even a quick breath.

"I wonder if he begrudges those seconds of silence," Mrs. Langston said wearily one evening. "Each time he starts off again, he barks a little faster, as if to make up for the time lost in breathing."

It was of little consequence, at first, when he began to bring home treasures found in his rambles. His first acquisition was an old mule bone that had been worn white and slick by time and weather. It was quite heavy, and the job of getting it home must have imposed something of a strain upon the enterprising young setter. He dragged his prize to the middle of the back yard, the gate being left open during much of the daytime, and sat proudly near it. His attitude was one of jealous ownership. Proof of this selfish sentiment came dramatically when the dominicker rooster wandered too close.

With a roar of hysterical rage the pup leaped for the rooster and bowled him over for a complete somersault.

The startled dominicker, ruffled and wide-eyed, squawked and raced for more civilized surroundings.

Growling fiercely, hackles bristling, Black Saddle returned to his vigil near the bone. He appeared entirely satisfied with his handling of the matter. For most of the remainder of that day he sat there, alert, waiting for further trespassing on the area that he considered hallowed by the bone. Only a hen or two had to be taught a lesson that day, and this was done by noise and threatening motions rather than by the kind of physical violence exerted on the rooster. This may have been out of deference to their sex.

Home from the field late that afternoon, Lee removed the bone from the back yard, lugged it out behind the barn, and hurled it into the sand ditch there. Black Saddle, who had followed, started after it, but Lee called him back scoldingly.

The pup tucked his tail and disappeared around the barn. He was clearly hurt and baffled by such treatment, and he must have felt that people have a strange, undependable sense of values. He lay until dark before his house, chin on paws, blinking slowly and ignoring Lee's efforts to cheer him up by offers to play.

"Now you've shattered his world," Mrs. Langston said dryly. "He has guarded that horrible thing all day, and now *purpose* has been removed from his life!"

Lee laughed. "It'll come back, I'll bet!"

This prediction proved correct. In fact, *purpose* came back into Black Saddle's life the very next day. He brought home a half-grown white Leghorn chicken that had been killed on the highway and laid it in approximately the same spot as the

Black Saddle was growling, showing his teeth

bone had occupied the day before. Then he sat near by and waited.

The morning warmed, and the moving sun found an opening directly above the pup, in the foliage of the chinaberry. For the next thirty minutes, until shade returned to that point, Black Saddle sat there, panting swiftly in the blazing spot of sunshine. He was obviously not one to abandon a strategic position when a worthy purpose was to be served.

Just before noon the big Langston tomcat, Buster, came from a cool sleep beneath the house, stretched slowly in magnificent laziness, rolled over, all motions carrying him nearer to the dead chicken.

Black Saddle growled softly, bristled. It was fair warning.

Buster looked at him with the contempt that age frequently lavishes upon immaturity. It had been like this since the puppy's arrival there. Until then, Buster had been the sole Langston pet, and he had no doubt seen in the pup the threat of competition. Eyes on the still, white Leghorn, he moved nearer.

Black Saddle was in a crouch now, growling steadily, showing his teeth. He was summoning up all the ferocity at his command. It was plain that he recognized this as a crisis, aware that the tomcat was much more to be respected than the dominicker rooster. Black Saddle had no remote desire to attack the cat, nor did he wish to lose his self-respect by sacrificing his rights to fear.

Lee and Mr. Langston came in from the field to dinner. First to reach the back-yard gate, Lee saw the grim tableau and motioned to his father.

Buster, filled with confidence and lithe power, was carefully ignoring the pup as he moved with swaying, lazy grace toward the Leghorn remains. In one swift instant that easy grace could change to blurring speed, with sharp claws slashing. No one knew this better than Black Saddle, for when he had been new at the Langston house the tomcat had slyly cuffed him with just enough unsheathed claw to inspire respect.

"He'd better learn about cats," Mr. Langston said. "Some day, he may meet up with a big bobcat down in the swamp."

Lee nodded. "Buster doesn't want that dead chicken. He just wants an excuse to slap the puppy."

Black Saddle let loose a wild roar, followed by hysterical barking, as if he thought some extra noise might impress and deter the cat. At the same time he moved in between the chicken and Buster.

The tomcat arched his back slightly and thrashed his long tail. He had turned almost sidewise to the pup, ready in case of attack to roll over on his back and send four sets of claws into a cruel attack.

But there was no attack. Black Saddle was willing to forego that risk and let the situation remain at the stalemate it had reached. His barks had subsided to a deep, steady growl as he waited for the cat to come closer—no doubt sending up earnest canine prayers that Buster would drop the matter and go about his business.

"He's scared," Mr. Langston said, "but he's going to stand on his rights."

Hearing the voice, for the man had made no effort to speak softly—Lee was sure he had intentionally broken the tableau— Buster looked toward the gate. Then he flicked his tail as if to say, "All this is quite beneath me," and turned away, dropping into his lazy, swaying gait.

"Buster might've slashed one of the pup's eyes," Mr.

Langston said, confirming Lee's suspicion. "Get the shovel and bury that chicken. Throw something heavy over the place so he won't dig the poor thing up."

While Lee was busy with this chore, Black Saddle watched disconsolately. He lay near by, panting, his mind likely busy with plans for the morrow. There must be something in the big, wide world that would be acceptable to people!

A disturbing thought occurred to Lee. Anyone seeing Black Saddle trotting down the highway, a limp chicken in his mouth, would promptly accuse him of being a chicken-killer. The word would get around, and some day Black Saddle might not come back home. One thing was certain: when field work let up a little, he and his father would build a pen for the setter.

During the next few days, the pup brought home a wide assortment of treasures: an old shoe, a sun-dried leather glove that must have been tossed aside during the previous winter, a shiny, new scythe for cutting yard grass—this last from Mrs. Wharton's place, Lee suspected. Black Saddle's most-prized acquisition seemed to be a faded pink girdle. From its appearance, the garment had but lately enjoyed use and had been washed and put out to dry.

With commendable haste Lee buried that, too.

Black Saddle was growing fast and beginning to feather out along rangy legs and tail. Alive with curiosity, he investigated everything that moved and many things that stayed still. He went to the field with Lee and Mr. Langston and spent much of his time in hunting along fence rows and in thickets, sniffing and snorting through grass and briars. Butterflies and grasshoppers he found especially appealing, and he raced after them, leaping and barking, his big ears flopping wildly. Having

wearied himself, he would retire to the coolest available shade
and sleep, building up strength for more grasshoppers and
butterflies, or for barking in the night.

One of his liveliest chases came when he flushed a half-
grown rabbit from the edge of a shallow drainage ditch over-
grown with dewberry vines. He gave this challenging project
his vocal all and disappeared in the creek bottom south of the
field. His frantic barking grew fainter and fainter, then died
away.

Lee stopped the tractor and yelled and whistled, but Black
Saddle paid no attention. This was something far greater and
more compelling than his master's voice. He was in the
shadowy woods, following a trail.

Almost two hours later, toward quitting time, the setter
returned to the field. He was panting hard, and he was wet
and muddy from stagnant sloughs. One ear was snagged by
a bramble; his muzzle was briar-ripped. But he had every
appearance of being happy. He barked little that night, even
at the late moon.

"You'd better arrange for him to chase a rabbit every afternoon," Mrs. Langston suggested at breakfast the next morning. "I slept last night, for a change."

"Runnin' rabbits ruins a bird dog," Lee objected. Then,
aware of the mistake he had made, he added, "It would spoil
him for what he's made to do, I mean."

His mother said nothing. She had taken her stand on the
bird-dog matter.

When Lee went out to feed Black Saddle that morning, the
pup was gone. He called and whistled. Once he thought he
heard him yipping excitedly down toward the creek, but he
couldn't be sure.

"He'll come back," Mr. Langston said from the back porch. "Your dog's just growing up, that's all."

On the way to the field that morning, Lee said, "Mama's still worried about the bird huntin'."

"When she makes up her mind about something important, it stays made up for a while," Mr. Langston told him. "It's just that she's trying to stand between you and danger." He paused to knock his pipe out on a locust fence post. "Right now, you're trying to stand between your pup and danger. You see how it is."

"I guess I do," Lee confessed. He thought about it as they walked along the winding field road. "While we're thinkin' like this," he said finally, "would be a good time to ask what you think about a pen for Black Saddle. It may be the best way to keep him out of trouble."

"The kind of wire you'd need for that comes pretty high," Mr. Langston reminded him. "Maybe we could put up a pair of stout posts and string a heavy wire between them, 'bout six feet off the ground. You can snap a long leash to it, and the pup can move about enough for exercise and stay home at the same time."

"It might work," Lee agreed, "but it'd be just like him to get the leash wrapped around one of the posts and then sit there all night, barkin'."

"He'll do that, all right," Mr. Langston said grimly. "We'll have to do something to keep him at home, with bird season coming on. He'll be an easy dog for somebody to steal, friendly as he is."

Lee hoped that Black Saddle would return to the field when the tractor started roaring, but at midmorning, when Mr. Langston had to leave for town, there was still no sign of the pup. Lee cut the tractor motor, sat listening for long minutes, but there was no sound of barking anywhere.

A half hour later, as he was making a turn to start back down the long cotton rows leading to the woods, Lee saw their car coming along the narrow road. His mother was at the wheel. He cut off the tractor again and waited for her to come up. In the silence this time he thought he heard a man yell somewhere down in the creek bottom.

Mrs. Langston pulled up and got out. She was carrying what looked like a wadded garment of some kind, and she was plainly excited.

"Your dog has just brought these home," she called, holding forth a pair of trousers. "You're lucky at least in one way: the man's billfold stayed in the hip pocket."

"Whose pants are they?" Lee asked weakly.

"I certainly have no idea," she said rather sharply, coming on toward him, brandishing the trousers as if to emphasize her feelings. "You'd better take these down to the creek and see who's trapped down there."

"You think that's it?" Lee gasped, seeing the prospect of trouble looming large.

"Who else but somebody in swimming would have left these pants where that crazy pup could steal them?" she asked.

Lee swallowed hard. There was logic in her question, but he dreaded facing Black Saddle's victim. "This is awful!" he said slowly, reaching a shaky hand to take the trousers.

"It really is— Listen, I heard someone yell off there. The poor fellow! Go on, Lee, take him his pants!"

Lee was sure she was laughing as she returned to the car, but he saw nothing funny in the business. Whoever was down there in the creek, caught in what must be a painfully awkward situation, would no doubt be pretty hot in the collar. Lee dreaded facing him.

Finding the man proved easy. Lee had gone only a short distance into the woods when he heard yells that carried a note of desperation.

"I'm comin'," he called back. Then he added, "Wait right there," which he realized was extremely silly advice to one who could do nothing else.

Rounding a bend in the low, clear stream, Lee saw the man standing dejectedly in waist-deep water. He was rather plump and very bald, and even at a distance Lee could see that he had sustained a painful sunburn.

Lee hurried, calling, "Why don't you get in the shade? You'll burn up there."

"I couldn't stay in the shade," the man called back hoarsely. "The mosquitoes chewed me to ribbons there. Hey, you've got my pants!" He started bankward.

"Yes, sir. Your billfold's still in 'em, too. I hope no change, or anything, got lost out—"

"I can spare the change," the man said. "Was that your pup? I tried to call him back, but—"

"He's only a few months old," Lee broke in, relieved to find the stranger in a better frame of mind than he had expected. "First time he's ever done a thing like this."

"I'll learn to hang my pants out of reach. Right pretty pup you have there, boy."

"Smart, too," Lee said with pride.

The rescued stranger's name was Dodson. He was visiting the Whartons. "I came down here for a swim," he said, clawing unhappily at mosquito welts on shoulders and chest. "Never got caught in such a mess before!"

"I never, either," Lee told him. "And I'm glad you're takin' it good-natured. Some men would be mighty upset at the pup and me and everybody else. I'm just awful sorry it happened."

Mr. Dodson smiled, but with an effort. "I'm a dog-lover, anyway. Maybe that's part of the reason I can take things like this and come up with a grin. Isn't that a Tomlin setter pup?"

"He is," Lee said with pride. "It was the runt of the litter, and Mr. Tomlin gave him to me back in the spring. He's the last male dog of the Tomlin line."

Mr. Dodson nodded appreciatively. "I thought he was a Tomlin. Hold onto him, boy. You've got a real treasure there."

"You like to bird hunt?"

"Love it. And I want to see that pup of yours in the field when he gets to be a grown dog."

"Fall after next, if you're down this way," Lee said, "I'll be glad to show you how he's shapin' up."

"Good. I'll be seeing you," Mr. Dodson promised.

After a few more minutes of such talk, Lee went back to the field and plowed to the homeward end of the rows. There he dismounted and headed for the house. He was eager to tell his mother how the trousers episode had turned out, and he was anxious to tie up Black Saddle before there was more trouble.

Mrs. Langston met him on the back porch. "When I came back to the house," she reported, "he was chasing a car down the highway, barking his silly head off."

Lee groaned. "That pup can scratch up more snakes than tie him up, some way."

I can stomp! Chasin' cars'll get him killed. I've just got to

"What did the man say?" his mother asked.

"He was mighty nice. Even said it was his fault for leavin' the pants where a pup could get at 'em. I'll go and find Black Saddle now."

But the phone rang just then, and Lee waited to learn whether or not the call concerned his enterprising pup.

He noted that his mother's face had gone white, and from her expression he judged that she was undergoing something of a verbal onslaught. At last she said, "I'm just awfully sorry, Mrs. Wharton. Lee will be right over." Then she hung up and turned slowly.

"You have just purchased two monogrammed sheets," she announced in a level tone. "They are rather expensive, I gather. Black Saddle has riddled them."

"Mrs. Wharton!" Lee groaned. "I'll bet that was her girdle, too!"

"I wouldn't be surprised. The sheets were on the line, drying. Go get him!"

Miserable, Lee left. He dreaded Mrs. Wharton. As he rounded the bend halfway to the Wharton place, he saw Black Saddle coming full tilt homeward. His long tongue was out, his big ears were laid back, and his eyes were wild with fright. His tail was tucked.

Lee slammed on brakes and yelled, but the pup paid him no mind. He was in panic, and he had one over-all purpose: to get home.

Chickens and a flock of bronze turkeys ranged the grove alongside the driveway up to the Wharton residence. A big gobbler, chest out, wings flared and scraping the ground, paraded in a showy strut, with now and then a clackety gobbling.

Lee pulled up to the porch just as the woman, obviously expecting him, emerged from the front door. She was heavy, and her firm face suggested a thundercloud.

"I'm sorry about the sheets," Lee began, "but he's just a pup—"

"It's come to a pretty pass," Mrs. Wharton cut in with feeling, "when a woman can't put out sheets and her personal —er—garments and expect to get them back! And in her own yard, at that!" She appeared deeply moved by the enormity of the thing. "Your crazy dog ruined the prettiest pair of sheets I had."

"I'll pay for 'em, Mrs. Wharton," Lee promised desperately. "How much were they worth? I'll get the money and—"

"I expect you to pay for them," she interrupted. "And I also expect you to pen up that—that *beast*—before he gets you into real trouble."

"Yes'm, I'm in enough trouble already." Lee could see the tatters of blue sheets hanging from a line beyond the corner of the house. "I guess you whacked him a good one, didn't you? I met him runnin' down the road, his eyes bucked wide . . ."

"I would have, but I couldn't get to him. The big bronze gobbler out there worked him over. He was beating the pup with his wings and stabbing him with his heavy bill. I thought your dog would never get loose, but it served him right."

"Yes'm," Lee said weakly. "It served him right, I guess."

❧ 3 ❧

BACK HOME FROM THE WHARTON PLACE, LEE FOUND THAT Black Saddle had retired to the doghouse. His clownish half-black, half-white face was more comical than ever. Lee thought he detected a look of shame in the pup's soft brown eyes.

"You ought to be lambasted!" he scolded. Then he knelt before the doghouse and laughed at the setter's contrite expression. Black Saddle refused to look up at him. Chin on paws, blinking slowly, he gazed studiedly past Lee and snuffled as if to say, "I'm not paying you any mind at all, boy."

Mrs. Langston came onto the back porch. "I've just talked with Mrs. Wharton, on the phone," she announced. "You owe her five dollars. The sheets were only three years old."

"They must've been pretty scrumptious to start with," Lee said sourly.

"Maybe it was the monogram," his mother suggested.

Before returning to the field after dinner, Lee brought a long rope from the barn and tied Black Saddle to the chinaberry tree. The pup would surely be too tired to bark after his busy day.

Lee and his father left the field earlier than usual that afternoon and returned to the house. They set two strong posts in

36

the back yard and strung a heavy wire between them. Then
Lee fastened a bridlesnap to the long rope, clipped the snap
onto the wire, and tied the other end of the rope to the dog's
collar. Black Saddle could range almost to the back porch in
one direction and to the back fence in the other. He could
go east and west, too, the snap sliding along the wire. It was
his first real imprisonment since arriving at the Langston
place.

When Lee left him there, the pup lunged after him, ready
to play and make up. But when he reached the end of the
rope, at mid-leap, he was snatched sharply backward by the
springiness of the taut wire, and he was being choked by the
tightened leather at his throat.

He scrambled up and tried it again, barking wildly for Lee
to come back and do something about it. Again he toppled
back. Yelping in angry confusion, he gained his feet and
shook himself.

Lee was watching him from just inside the back door. He
wanted to go back and pet the puzzled victim of human in-
genuity. It was bad that he couldn't explain everything to the
pup. Lee felt a hot lump forcing into his throat, but it went
away when Black Saddle began barking wildly in a hysteria
of mixed pleading and scolding.

Lee hurried into the kitchen and gathered up a pile of saved
table scraps with which to buy silence. But Black Saddle was
not interested in making a deal. All he wanted right then was
loose. He lunged for the boy, reared up on him, tried to lick
his face. He was yipping and whining and begging as never
before. He refused to look at a proffered bone.

Now he was running a circle, and Lee suddenly realized
that the rope was wrapping tightly about his legs. Black Saddle

was bellowing and lunging around and around, tail thrashing madly. Lee stooped and clawed at the rope just as the setter lunged again for him. They went down together.

"Hey!" Lee whooped. "Get offa me!"

"Not 'offa,' " Mrs. Langston corrected him from the edge of the porch. "You should say *off* me. Even in emergencies one should use good English."

"This is no time for a lesson, Nell!" Mr. Langston said gruffly as he moved past her and down the steps and headed for the mixture of boy and dog.

Lee had managed to catch hold of Black Saddle's collar and stave off at least part of the affectionate onslaught. With his other hand he was tugging at the rope.

"Mercy, Hurd, which one's the setter?" Mrs. Langston asked.

"It's the other dog," Lee told her. "The one with the pedigree."

"Oh, that clears it up. You're just the last Langston." Then she went back into the house.

During supper that evening, they could hear the metal snap scraping and rattling along the wire as Black Saddle ranged back and forth. He appeared to be working hard at solving the combination. For a time, after the excitement with Lee, the setter had been quiet; then as the fact of his imprisonment had become more apparent, and as the rope had wrapped around an end post, shortening the scope of his operations, he had begun to bark, with now and then a longdrawn howl for emphasis.

Lee went out at last with the flashlight and found him sitting by the involved post. His air was one of sadness and dejection. When Lee caught his collar and led him around and around the post, unwinding the leash, Black Saddle kept his tail tucked tight, and he cringed with every movement.

When the rope had been cleared from the post, Lee led the pup to the doghouse and shoved him into it, saying, "Go to bed! Get quiet!"

But Black Saddle had no remote intention of being quiet. He shot forth from the doghouse door, barking and begging. Lee sprinted for the back steps and barely escaped being hobbled again.

As the night wore on, one thing became increasingly clear: A pen must be built for the setter.

Early the next morning Lee and his father drove to town for a roll of heavy poultry wire and some staples. By noon they had built the pen, cupping the wire to the inside at the bottom and burying it as a means of preventing the pup from scratching out. Inside the gate, where such cupping was not possible, they buried two widths of one-by-ten oak planks. The gate would be as high as the fence, which was, roughly, six feet, and it would be fastened by a strong hook at the bottom as well as at a point near the top.

After dinner they tied Black Saddle in the bed of the pickup and drove toward the Tomlin place. Mr. Langston was as eager as Lee to show the old man how the runt had grown.

"Mr. Tomlin may want him back," Mrs. Langston had said. "Can I be optimistic about this thing?"

"Don't pay her any mind," Mr. Langston had said quietly to Lee. "She's as crazy about Sad as you are."

"I'm not *that* crazy," she had protested with considerable feeling.

On the way to the Tomlin place, Lee said abruptly, "Let's

do call him 'Sad.' It sounded just right when you said it a while ago."

"Suits me," Mr. Langston agreed. "It doesn't quite fit the pup, but it'll be an easy name to call."

They reached the Tomlin place in early afternoon and found the old man on the front porch, eating a watermelon.

"Come on in," he called, waving his butcher knife. "That you, Hurd?"

"Yes, sir. We thought we'd show you something. Untie Sad, Lee."

"Hey, what've you got there?" Mr. Tomlin called when Sad leaped from the truck. He wiped the long knife along his overalls leg and came toward the steps, his eyes on the setter. "Here, boy!" he invited the pup.

Sad bounded up the steps, answering the summons as if trained to it.

"Well, I do believe he knows me!" the old man said happily, stroking Sad's broad head and tugging lightly at his sleek ears. "Now, he's a fine one, ain't he! You'd never guess he was the runt. Look at them legs an' that chest! You all have seats."

Soon they were bringing Mr. Tomlin up to date on the last Tomlin. Lee was doing most of the talking, happy over the old man's pleasure. "I named him Black Saddle," he finished.

"It's a good name, but what'll you call him?"

"Sad," Lee told him. "It'll be easy to call him by. Say, do you have any anti-barkin' pills?"

Old man Tomlin laughed. "You might try a big dose of strychnine. That's about the only thing that'll stop a Tomlin setter from barkin'. Maybe it makes 'em deepchested an' gives 'em the lung power they're famous for. You'll just have to put up with his barkin', I reckon."

"He chased a rabbit yesterday," Lee said with pride. "We were down in the field and—"

"Good!" Mr. Tomlin cried. "Butterflies, grasshoppers an' rabbits. That's about the usual pattern." He looked out into the grove, where the pup was racing about, investigating brush piles and clumps of growth. "Just so he *chases*; that's the main thing." The old man's blue eyes were squinted as he watched Black Saddle in motion. "He moves pretty. Look at that tail, thrashin' from side to side. Ten or 'leven years back, that could be ol' Saddle. He looked like that, an' he moved the very same way."

This kind of talk lasted for perhaps an hour. It might have lasted all afternoon if Mr. Langston hadn't asked about Mary Lou.

For the better part of a minute the old man gave no sign of having heard the question. His eyes were on the setter, his face expressionless except for the extra busy-ness of his thick brows. Finally he said, still watching Black Saddle, "I just don't know, Hurd. I don't know how she is. She an' that thing she married don't ever come aroun' me."

"Now, that's bad," Mr. Langston said easily. "When a girl's gran'pa invites her to his house, she ought to come."

"They haven't been invited," the old man snapped. "An' they won't be—"

"Well, that being the case," Mr. Langston interrupted, "I can't say I blame Mary Lou and Embry for staying away. She's a fine girl, Mr. Tomlin."

"She *was*." And, to change the painful subject, "By the way, I didn't send that mama dog to Chicago, along with the pups."

"You're keepin' her?" Lee asked.

"No, I sold her to a man named Dodson. This is the first

time in seventy-five years there hasn't been a dog on this place."

"Dodson?" Lee asked with excitement. "Was he a heavy-set, sunburned fellow."

"That fits him to a T," Mr. Tomlin replied. "What do you know about the fellow?"

Lee gave a full account of the trousers episode. "And it turns out to be a mighty small world," he finished. "Mr. Dodson now owns the mama of the pup that stole his pants!"

Mr. Tomlin laughed shortly. "He'll hang 'em high next time, I bound you!"

As they rode homeward, Mr. Langston said, "Maybe I shouldn't've asked about Mary Lou, but it's just ornery stubbornness that makes things the way they are. That poor old fellow ought to be ashamed of himself."

Summer moved into fall, with cotton opening and ears of corn, tan-husked, pointing groundward, awaiting harvest. Cool nights came, and dry, bright days. Came also the opening of school, after which Lee had little time for Sad. Saturdays were busy with cotton-picking and with trips to the gin. The crop was good.

Now and then, at twilight, Lee went out to the pen and played with the pup, tossing a ball or a stick for him to retrieve. It was a game of endless delight to Sad, who bounded out eagerly for whatever was thrown, then brought it back with high-headed pride. Patiently, Lee taught him to rear up, feet against his master's chest, and deliver what he had retrieved.

When he thought Sad had learned his lesson well, Lee took his father out to the pen for a demonstration.

"He does a good job of *this*," Mr. Langston said, nodding

with appreciation, "but he may not tie it up with a dead bird. I've been through this business with a pup or two."

"But it's a step *toward* retrievin'," Lee insisted.

"I guess so, but there's something about a limp, warm bird, or a crippled one, that makes a green pup do some mighty silly things."

"What?" Lee wanted to know.

"No telling. You'll just have to wait and see how Sad's affected. He may snap right into retrieving without a bobble, and then again, he may carry on like a plumb half-wit!"

"It'll soon be bird season," Lee said, lowering his voice and giving a quick glance toward the house. "What'll we do about it when the time comes?"

"I just don't know, son." The words were slow with thinking. "You see, I promised your mother, back when Joe's eye was shot out, that I'd never hunt again. She hasn't forgotten that promise."

"But it's not fair to hold you to it now."

The man said nothing for a long moment. "No, it's not quite fair now, I guess, but we'll have to be understanding about this thing. A woman loves her own, and she wants safety for them."

"But we'd be careful," Lee declared. "Just because somebody was shot accidentally before I was born, I may never have a gun 'til I'm grown!"

"We'll try to work it out better than that," his father said. "Stop feeling sorry for yourself, an' let's go in and eat supper."

Lee knew his father had a problem, caught as he was between two loyalties and two responsibilities. Maybe it was bad to grow up and be faced with the need to make difficult decisions in connection with responsibilities.

Sad, fast becoming tall and rangy, was often restless in his pen. He trotted around the wire, some days, around and around, stopping here and there to rear up on it. Watching the setter, Lee was sure the time would come when he would try to leap the wire, which was about five feet high, approximately a foot having been lost by the cupping-in of the mesh at the bottom. Lee was sure that Sad, with a running start and a climbing jump, could carry himself right over. And, once out of the confining pen, the setter would really go places. He had been imprisoned for a long time, and his muscles were crying out for use. And now, close to the opening of the bird season, Sad might never get back home.

On the following Saturday morning Lee and his father strung a strand of barbed wire, tight, a few inches above the poultry wire. Sad followed them about, barking frequent advice or bringing sticks to Lee for more of the game, of which he never tired.

On the next Wednesday night a cool wind blew in from the north, and fall was in the air. If the wind quieted, there would be frost. When Lee went to bed, the wind was still coming in sharp gusts that set up varied tones of weird whistling about the eaves.

Faintly, at first, came the music of the hounds. They were far off, up the creek bottom. Lee slipped from bed, raised his north window and leaned out to listen. He had always sensed a deep thrill on hearing hounds follow a hot trail at night. He thought of them vaguely as almost disembodied voices plunging through the darkness, pulled by the elusive magnet of scent that led out in front somewhere to the desperate wild thing they chased. The pack was moving fast down the creek bottom, their voices rising and falling in a tricky cadence that sent a prickly sensation along the back of the boy's neck.

"A fox chase!" he whispered and leaned farther out as if the inches gained would help him to catch more of the music that lay in the tangle of hound voices.

Somewhere along the edge of the bottom there were men on horses, in cars and trucks, men dedicated to the ancient sport. They were following along the edge of the ridge, hearing their hounds . . . and this listening was their only reward. Each man could pick from the swiftly changing fabric of sound the voice of his own hound, or hounds. Each man knew which hound had struck the trail, which hound was now in the lead. Each man, just from the baying and bugling of the hounds, could visualize the distribution of the pack racing headlong through the darkness of the deep woods.

Now Sad was answering the hounds, no doubt envying them their freedom and glory in being able to follow the trail that was their heritage. The nearer the hounds drew toward a point in the creek bottom nearest the Langston place, the more impassioned were his barks and whines.

"He's really talkin' to 'em!" Lee whispered. "He's sayin', 'Wait for me! Let me go with you. I wasn't born to chase a fox, but I'll help you!' "

It was right pitiful, Lee thought, to be penned up and to hear free dogs racing through the woods, following their keen noses, which were locked in on a sly, wild wraith called "fox."

"*Whooooo-EEEeee!*" cried a far-off, chase-happy hunter.

"And they don't even want the fox!" Lee marveled. "They'd lose a chance at another race if they caught the fox."

It was a strange kind of hunting, in which the hunters lose

if they capture what they chase. To be really successful, they must fail! It was the first time Lee had ever thought of this, and he pondered it. He tried to think of some other kind of hunting in which this was true, but he had no success at all.

The hounds passed on, sweeping southward, their voices growing fainter. Lee turned from the window, back to his bed. Then something stopped him and he froze there, listening. It was like the stopping of a clock, scarcely heard in its regular ticking, but deafening in meaningful silence when the pendulum is stilled.

There was no sound from Sad.

Lee stood very still and strained to hear another whine from the pen, but none came. The night was empty, save for the dying-away voices of the hounds.

Having dressed quickly, Lee caught up his flashlight and slipped downstairs. Out the back door, he leaped from the porch and sprinted for the pen. The beam of his flashlight raked the gate and streaked along the fence as soon as Lee was within range of the enclosure. He reached the corner of the pen nearest the gate and called, "Sad! *Sad!*"

But the setter did not come bounding from his house, barking and whining in delight.

Lee opened the gate and went in, playing the beam along the fence as he sought some clue to Sad's point of departure. Finally, on the back of the pen, the light picked up a tag of white hair clinging to a barb of the top wire.

Lee went to it and felt the white blob, to make sure it was not a tag of cotton or of paper left there by careless wind. No, it was coarse hair from Sad.

There was no need to call. Sad was at that moment racing toward the creek bottom, every muscle alive and straining to catch the hounds. So long penned up, now gloriously free, the setter was likely streaking down a starlit cotton row, his ears laid back, his eyes wild with happiness, as he lunged toward the clear bugling of the fox-drawn hounds.

Lee stood there for a long moment, fingering the tag of hair. Then he said softly, "I reckon I don't much blame him."

A light came on in the downstairs bedroom as Lee walked slowly back toward the house. When he went up the back porch steps, his father called, "Sad must've got out. I don't hear him barking any more."

"He jumped the fence," Lee said calmly. "He's gone."

"It was a good jump." Then Mr. Langston yawned. "He'll come back. Go on to bed, Lee."

Getting back to bed was no particular problem, but Lee found that he couldn't go to sleep. This was the very thing he had dreaded, Sad's escape at night. No telling where he'd wind up now, with those wide-ranging hounds, which were sometimes found as far as fifteen miles from where they had started. Sometimes it took days to round them all up again. Maybe it was the very bigness of the thing that was part of the thrill in fox hunting. This was not a beagle at a sinkhole, clawing for a scared rabbit. This was hunting on the grand scale, with miles of the country involved.

Lee rose and went to the window. He listened for a long time, to catch some sound of the chase. Off there, somewhere deep in the creek bottom, he knew the hounds were still in hot pursuit of the fox. And with them, screaming his heart out, was Sad, son of old Saddle, who had hunted whatever his master had wanted him to hunt, day or night.

Lee hoped the fox would double back, as foxes often do, and bring the dogs in a general retracing upstream. He wondered if he could hear Sad's bellowing mingled with the voices of the hounds.

Then a strange thinking set in: A boy raising a dog is much like a father raising a son; he feeds him, protects him, trains him, and the more he does wrong, the more the boy loves him and tries to make him better. The boy looks to the future and hopes that when his dog grows up he will know how to do the things he's supposed to do.

And then one day, or one night—puppy or boy, for Lee was carrying on the parallel—he flies the safety of home. It's a big world out there, calling him. People say it's because he has spirit that he went away, and they say that he would be no good without spirit, but the one responsible worries and frets and hopes.

"It's the Sunday-school story of the prodigal son!" Lee said softly. And he lay there in his bed and thought about it, for he could not sleep. Then, to comfort himself, he added, "And the prodigal son came home!"

And since the hour was fit for nothing but thinking, the boy lay there and let his mind ramble. The world was dark and silent, and the time was made for thinking. The gusty wind still came and went, with weird moanings about the eaves. Now and then, from the hearth of the fireplace in Lee's room, a cricket chirped as if gloating over security achieved with winter approaching.

A rooster crowed in the distance, advertising dawn. A turkey gobbled, perhaps the very one that had whipped Sad over at Mrs. Wharton's that summer day. A tractor roared along the highway, pulling a rumbling trailer-load of cotton, heading for the early line-up at the gin. The day was coming alive.

Lee got up and dressed. Downstairs, he found his father

busy with getting coffee started. Lee could tell that he hadn't rested well.

"We'd better put up another piece of barbed wire on that pen fence," Lee said easily, as if he had no doubt that Sad would return home.

Mr. Langston nodded, yawned. "I wonder how he made out, playing foxhound last night."

"Chances are he had a good time," Lee said dryly.

At breakfast, Mrs. Langston's only comment was, "That mixed-up dog had better decide what kind he is."

Lee had no comment on that. He was sure that his mother was just as worried as he and his dad were.

"Don't let this get your mind off your schoolwork," Mr. Langston warned. "We'll get the dog back, all right. I'll be asking around to find out who was fox hunting last night. It's likely that Sad took up with one of the hounds and is now visiting with his new friend."

"When you go asking around," Mrs. Langston suggested casually, "you might tell the hunters that the Langston hound has curly hair and well-feathered legs."

At school that day, Lee tried to keep his mind on English and math and history and science, but they had suddenly become trivial and unrelated to the real values of life. No matter how hard he tried to concentrate, the question of Sad's whereabouts persistently pushed all academic matters aside. Two teachers scolded him for not paying attention. Miss Weston, whose very life was Algebra I, took his inattention very seriously.

"Lee," she said icily and in a much sharper tone than she commonly used, "I've asked you three times to tell me what x should represent in this problem. Please answer the question."

"Yes'm," Lee said, flushing and bringing her into focus against the blackboard. "I—"

"There is no 'yes'm' in the problem," she broke in. "We cannot let x stand for that. You were not listening."

"Yes'm," Lee admitted, swallowing hard. "I'm sorry, Miss Weston."

She nodded, made a quick notation in her gradebook, and said curtly, "See me after class."

"Yes'm." Lee slumped deep in his desk, succeeding in concealing most of himself behind Alice Jessup, who had giggled just audibly enough to let him know that she was enjoying his predicament. He had no intention of letting Miss Weston see how hard he was blinking to hold back tears.

But maybe the teacher had seen how close he was to a show of feeling; otherwise she would have insisted on a full treatment of the x matter. Miss Weston was not one to pass over things easily. When he stopped at her desk on the way out, he would tell her that she hadn't hurt his feelings, that he had deserved even more than she had said to him. He would tell her why he was so worried and why he had devoted most of the period to looking out the south window of the classroom.

When the bell rang, Alice turned instantly and whispered, "She's going to get you, Lee!" She seemed to relish the idea.

"I like you, too!" Lee snapped.

Miss Weston was standing very straight at her desk, her slender face impassive, as she watched Lee moving slowly forward, giving the others time to get out of the room. "Come ahead," she called. "My next class will be here in a moment."

"Yes'm. Look, Miss Weston, I'm mighty sorry—"

"Of course you are," she cut in, but there was less of an edge to her voice than there had been when she had scolded him. "This is the first time you've been inattentive in my class. What reason do you have to offer?"

"My dog got out last night," Lee told her.

"Out of what?"

"His pen. He jump-climbed a five-foot fence with barbed wire on top and took off after a pack of foxhounds."

"And your mind was on your dog instead of algebra," Miss Weston summed it up.

"Yes'm. I've had him since he was a wobbly pup. He's a black-and-white setter, one of the Tomlin dogs."

"Indeed?" Miss Weston appeared interested in this fact. "I had Mary Lou Tomlin in algebra."

"Her grandpa gave me the pup," Lee told her, happy to find this common ground between them. "He's mighty smart and pretty—the pup is, I mean," he finished awkwardly.

The teacher stopped a quick smile. "I thought you were describing the puppy," she said. "I've met Mr. Luke Tomlin. You may go, Lee, and don't let this sort of thing happen again."

"Yes'm." He left Miss Weston's room in haste and gratitude.

Alice Jessup was poking along the corridor. When Lee started past her, she called, "What'd she do? She threaten you with the office?"

"We talked about a dog," he said over his shoulder, and left her there, confused and tortured by seething curiosity.

It was a long day for Lee Langston. He assured himself over and over that Sad would be back home, in his pen, barking at the school bus when it pulled up at the Langston place. Then, after each of these surges of optimism, Lee warned himself to be ready for disappointment. It was a day of suspense.

Long before the bus began slowing down to let Lee out, he had moved to the front. He could see the pen, where Sad would likely be if he had made his way home, but there was no sign of the setter. Then, as the bus stopped, he had a full view of the front yard and of the house, but Sad was nowhere in sight.

Mr. Langston came onto the front porch as Lee entered the gate. From his air Lee gathered that no good word awaited. "Heard any news?" he called, trying to sound casual.

"Not a thing. Oh, I did hear that the Willdon boys were hunting last night. We'll go up to their place Saturday unless Sad turns up before then."

"Saturday's a long time off," Lee reminded him.

"Your name and address are on the dog's collar. If Sad *was* stolen, there's no use going anywhere to ask about him. If he's with some fox hunter, we'll hear by Saturday. You can't stay out of school to hunt for him."

Friday was much like Thursday. Of course, Lee was very alert in Miss Weston's algebra—an attitude that doubtless brought keen disappointment to Alice Jessup. Lee was determined not to be optimistic, for he had learned that this makes disappointment keener when it must be faced.

Back home, he found that no word of the dog had come. His mother made him feel a little better that evening when she said, "In spite of how I've talked, I hope we haven't seen the last of the last Tomlin."

4

ON SATURDAY MORNING LEE AND MR. LANGSTON WENT TO SEE Mr. Ad Willdon, who lived five miles up the creek.

"Sure didn't see a setter that night," the farmer told them. "He might've run with the houn's, far's that goes. Was your name an' address on the collar?"

"It was stamped good and clear in the metal," Lee assured him. "Did all your dogs come home?"

"We rounded ever' one of 'em up by two o'clock that night, I figger it was," Mr. Willdon said. "Our dogs come to the horn pretty good. Oh, by the way, I did hear that one of Harve Dowdy's dogs didn't come in 'til the next evenin'. You might go up the creek an' talk with Harve."

Having thanked Mr. Willdon, they drove to the Dowdy place, almost two miles farther up the creek.

"My ol' Blue come in by hisself," the lank farmer told them. "You say yore dog's a black-an'-white setter?"

"Yes, sir, he's a big, rangy one, but he won't be a year old 'til spring. He's not trained at all, so he won't be any good for huntin' this season."

The man shook his head sorrowfully and bit off a large hunk of dry twist tobacco, which he shifted from side to side of his mouth as if to aid concentration. "Any feller that'd steal a lost dog wouldn't know that, though, 'til bird season opened.

53

If he saw the pup had good stuff, he might keep him an' train him for next year. If'n a real scoun'l picked him up, he'd sell the dog an' git whut he could."

"If you hear anything," Mr. Langston put in, "let us know. We don't want to lose that dog."

"Sure will, Hurd. I sure will." Mr. Dowdy was walloping his twist into a comfortable quid by this time. "I ain't got a smidgen of patience with anybody'll steal a dog."

They drove on back home. Lee was trying not to show how worried he was, but there was a deep-down, hollow, lost feeling in him. From Wednesday night to Saturday noon is a long time, and suspense had been mounting steadily. Since his escape from the pen, Sat must have almost starved! But surely he had gone to some farmhouse and begged food; or, falling back on instinct, he had caught and killed a chicken to satisfy his wild hunger. This inspired a deeper fear: a strange dog caught killing chickens would be shot down like a mad dog! Lee bit his lip and tried to put this dismal thought out of his mind.

"Don't think the worst 'til you've got to," Mr. Langston said quietly, eyes on the winding road.

"No, sir," Lee said, jerking from his grim reverie. Many times he had been surprised like this by his father, who seemed to have a mysterious way of sensing Lee's thoughts. "Maybe it seems a lot longer than it really has been since Sad got away."

"Well, it's been a long time, all right." Mr. Langston cleared his throat lightly. "In raising a dog or a wild pet, you always have to be ready to face the worst. A dog's going to be a dog, and the more he has of the hunting instinct, the more things he'll do to worry you."

"And the more he's worth to you," Lee added. "It sort of balances up the good and the bad. The better dog he is, the more trouble he is."

"That says it pretty well," Mr. Langston agreed, nodding. "If a pet never gave you any trouble, he wouldn't get as deep into you as he ought. I guess we value such things according to how much we spend on 'em . . . not in money, but in love an' work an' worry, an' in whatever else we spend on 'em."

They drove on for a piece before Lee said, "I wish Sad didn't love a car so much, 'specially a pickup truck. It'll make him easy to catch and carry off somewhere."

"Most bird dogs are like that. Just wait'll he rides a few times to hunting ground. Whatever he rides in will stand for the very thing he loves most: the chance to find birds. He'll go wild every time the motor starts . . . just as he will whenever he sees a shotgun or a hunting coat."

Now the boy's mind rambled in a tangle of hopes and fears. He saw himself with a new gun and dressed in a new khaki hunting coat, with Sad racing and wheeling about him, begging for a hunt. It was a beautiful picture. . . .

Then two adverse possibilities clouded it: 1. What if his mother remained firm in her stand against hunting? 2. What if they never again saw the rangy, happy-natured setter? Lee swallowed hard and tried to think of something else.

"I know just about how you feel," Mr. Langston said quietly. "Once I had a Gordon setter. I was about grown then, I reckon it was. I lent him to a neighbor, who had a cousin out from Memphis and wanted an extra dog that day. Mine was on point in some high grass, when a single streaked up right toward him, flying low. The visitor shot and missed the bird. But he shot my Gordon right in the side and killed him instantly." The man shrugged. "That's how things go sometimes."

"That was awful," Lee said, realizing how trite the remark must sound. "The fellow paid for your dog, I guess."

"Offered to, but I didn't want any pay. Some things money won't replace. I'd raised the Gordon from a pup."

Lee wondered if his father was mercifully trying to prepare him for the worst. Being a man, he was aware of how, in the process of growing up, one must be ready to meet reversals and endure them. Now he was telling his son in a gentle, roundabout way that he, too, must be prepared to face loss and sorrow and have the strength to adjust to them when necessary. Lee wondered if this account of the ill-fated Gordon was a subtle means of toughening him and of preparing him for the grief that might lie ahead.

They rode in silence the rest of the way home. Lee's eyes were busy searching the hills and valleys for some vagrant flash of white against distant growth. Sad could be just anywhere, seeking his way back home. Once he thought he saw a big dog in the distance, a white-and-black dog, and he caught his breath sharply, straining his eyes to bring out the true shape of a dog against the dead brush and growth. Then he saw that it was a low stump partly shielded by a tangle of briars. Where the dark-brown bark had peeled away, the dead wood was white.

Lee was sure of one thing: if Sad never came back, he would not want another dog. There could never be another like Sad, who had been so briefly a runt. There could never be another Sad, so long-legged and heavy-shouldered at six months, so big-footed, wide-eared, so insatiably curious and so affectionate. It would be impossible, Lee was sure, for any other dog to mean as much to him as Sad had meant. He could not be replaced.

They were following the dirt road along the creek valley. Pines and oaks stood in dark clumps, relieving the vista of sedge. Growths of sumac, their seed-heads darkening into the crimson spires they would be in autumn, were like soft shadows against the waist-high grass. Now and then they crossed a narrow bridge over some sand-run leading toward the creek. Sassafras, with leaves speckling toward fall, fringed the fence rows. It was bird country.

As they came in sight of the grove of oaks and pecans which sheltered the house, Mr. Langston said, "There's one big thing in our favor."

"What's that?" Lee asked eagerly.

"There are a great many honest people. Only a very few men out of all we know would try to beat you out of your dog."

When they went into the house, Mrs. Langston called from the kitchen, "Lee, you got a card in the mail this morning. Look on the mantel."

Something in her tone made Lee hurry. But there was no power on earth that could have hastened his reading of the outlandish scrawl penciled on the postal card:

Come and git yore setar we caint fill him up an we caint sleap fer him ballin an haowlin all nite. we have got him tide up.

yrs.
Jody Lamb

ps. We are on the Medders place ease of Wadley.

"It's about Sad!" Lee yelled to his father. "He's over near Wadley. Where's that?"

" 'Bout eight miles down the creek," Mr. Langston answered, hurrying in. "Come on, boy!" And, to Mrs. Langston, "We'll eat when we get back."

"An' save me a thick steak off the fatted calf," Lee called back.

They left her there, the noon meal dished up and ready for the table. "They're both about Sad's age!" she said slowly, outdone. "Fatted calf?" She went to the window and watched them whip away in the pickup. "*Fatted—* Oh, that blessed boy!"

Wadley was a nigh-deserted sawmill town on the edge of the creek bottom. When they had arrived there via a rough graveled road, they turned left and followed a deeply rutted swamp way that wandered tortuously eastward. This finally led to the Meadows place and to the run-down shack of Mr. Jody Lamb.

"Yonder's Sad!" Lee cried, pointing.

The setter, having recognized the truck, was lunging and bellowing. The top of the hickory sapling to which he was tied was thrashing violently.

Five little Lambs, unwashed and uncombed, were playing about the woodpile in the front yard. At sight of the truck bearing strangers toward them, they raced for the house and crowded through the small front door, scrambling and fighting to beat each other into the security awaiting there. Within seconds their pinched faces, eyes and mouths wide, appeared at the lone front window.

Mr. Jody Lamb came forth to meet the visitors. He wore patched overalls that flapped loosely about his long, thin

Sad was lunging and whining

legs, and his blue denim work-shirt, repaired and faded, was too big at all points. A droop-brimmed black felt hat completed the illusion of a live scarecrow. He moved with a shambling gait, unplanned and careless.

"Well, howdy," Mr. Lamb greeted the two. His voice was thin and high-pitched. "Y'all must've come fer the dog. I tied him up an' putt some turphentime on his cuts Thursday mornin'. 'Course, I fed 'im, too. Lordy, that dog et! He was empty plum' down to his heels."

Lee went on ahead, losing the rest of Mr. Lamb's eager report. Before untying the rope, he caught Sad's collar firmly, saying, "Be still, boy!" The words hurt a little, for the hot lump had suddenly crowded back into his throat.

Sad was lunging and whining in a determined struggle to get at Lee's face. His thick tail, matted with mud and cockleburs, thrashed swiftly from side to side. His ears, which were heavy with mud and burs and dried blood, did not flop as easily as usual. From tip to tip the setter was scratched and scored, his curly coat discolored with the gummy mud and silt of the creek bottom.

"What do we owe you?" Mr. Langston asked the swamp dweller.

"Aw, I wouldn't charge a neighbor fer helpin' him out like this," the man said. "Hit's like the Golden Rule out of the Bible says, an' that's how I try to live. 'Course, the dog et pretty heavy, an' all that."

"We'd rather pay you somethin'," Lee interrupted. "You took trouble an' doctored him an' fed him, an'—"

"Well, hit was jes' cornbread an' some coon bones an' gravy we had lef' from breakfast," Mr. Lamb pointed out modestly. "After that, hit was jes' table scraps, like cornbread an' pot-likker from collards. Whutever I give him, he shore et it! An' 'spec' I used a half a bottle of turphentime on him. Ain't nothin' like turphentime fer cuts."

"You could have fed your pigs on what the dog ate, couldn't you?" Mr. Langston inquired, bringing his wallet into view.

"Well, I've got two pigs, but they're roamin' the bottom, feedin' on acorns an' slough fish an' whutever snakes they kin ketch." The man eyed the wallet with a swift glance. His manner was somewhat like that of a gaunt crane eager for breakfast on a shallow sand bar, viewing an unwary minnow that approaches within range of his swift, sharp bill.

"Would five dollars pay you for your trouble?" Mr. Langston inquired, bringing forth a bill.

"Hit would, now, shore! Like I say, I try to live by the Golden Rule out of the Bible. Hit's the best way." He took the bill and fingered it as if enjoying the soft, solid texture of the paper. "I always try to be a good neighbor. By the way, you got any cigarette makin's? I'm plum' out."

"No papers," Mr. Langston told him, "but I've some pipe tobacco."

"I got papers." He took the proffered can, started to pour tobacco into the palm of his hand.

"Keep the can," Mr. Langston said. "I've some more at home."

"Well, now, you're a gentleman!" Mr. Lamb pocketed the tin quickly as if he feared the offer might be withdrawn.

Sad was clearly happy to be back in his pen. He frisked about, sniffing and snorting along every foot of the fence and about the doghouse. His thoroughness made Lee wonder if he was trying to determine whether or not there had been trespassers during his absence.

That afternoon Lee and his father stretched another strand of barbed wire above the first one. That would surely hold him.

Lee spent the late afternoon in removing burs and briars from the setter's curly coat, which had thickened with the coming of cold weather. And, while the afternoon sun was still warm, he bathed the dog, rinsed him free of soap, then rubbed him hard with an old, coarse towel.

Proving his gratitude, Sad promptly rolled in the dust and shook himself thoroughly. Having taken care of this ritual, he stretched out and went to sleep, snuffling in deep contentment.

"Man," Mrs. Langston said at supper that evening, "is dog's best friend . . . and that's truer than it is original!"

On Monday afternoon Lee raced in from the school bus, changed clothes hurriedly and headed out the back door.

"Where in the world are you going?" his mother called.

"To take Sad for a run." Lee carefully avoided the word "hunt."

"Oh," she said briefly.

As he opened the gate of the pen, Lee was unaware that his mother was standing at the window of the back bedroom, watching.

They went along the pasture fence, then bore off to the right toward a crimson sumac thicket. Lee knew that quail fed along there, and he watched Sad race out ahead, barking and leaping. When Sad stopped and looked back, Lee waved him on, as he had seen bird hunters do. As if understanding the motion, Sad bounded ahead a few yards, then stopped and looked back, waiting. His manner seemed to say, "Come on, you run, too. It's fun!"

Sad wheeled and struck out again, ears flopping, tail thrashing furiously. It was a marvelous, cool, long-shadowed world of fragrances and mysterious scents. The red sun hung low above the creek bottom to the southwest. Just above the tree-tops and to the left of the sun, a ragged line of mallards made a soft gash against the pale sky.

In the goings and comings of ducks and geese, Lee Langston had always found a deep, moving beauty. He couldn't put it into words, but there was a glory far more thrilling than words in the fall and spring migrations. The geese were more meaningful, he thought, than the ducks, many of which spent the winter along the creek. The Canada honkers, though, went on over to the Mississippi River and chose some quiet, sequestered sand bar for their southern retreat. Each year, Lee had read, they returned to the same bar unless hunted there too much; and each spring they went back to the same nesting-ground in Canada. They *knew*, somehow. Man needs roads and signs and all manner of aids to get him from one distant place to another, but a duck or a goose merely streaks into the limitless sky, sets his course, fans the air with tireless wings and goes where his built-in wisdom takes him!

Sad was standing still, looking back at Lee. His tail was swinging excitedly from side to side. Lee waved again, and the dog moved on, changing his course to sharp left. He held his head high and trotted stiff-leggedly.

Lee's heart raced, and he breathed fast. He knew as little about bird hunting as Sad, but he sensed that the dog's keen nose had caught some wonderful, exciting scent. It *must* be quail.

Out of the mingled odors of life and of growth, which lay in an invisible blanket imperceptible to man, just above the cooling ground, there was only one scent really satisfying to a bird dog: *quail.* Sad was learning now, and he had a great deal to get straightened out. Other birds had left their trails along here, and their odors rode the drifting north breeze. Sad must learn, with the aid of marvelous instinct, which was the right, *true* scent. Just as a boy must learn through training and trial and error to detect the false, to distinguish between the *real* and the *almost real*, so must Black Saddle, the last Tomlin, learn.

Lee watched the setter, now stealing in a crouch through the sedge. Once or twice he had seen a covey of quail feeding in deep grass at sunset, and he knew what a tangle of crisscross trails they must leave. He looked ahead of the dog for some sign of the brown birds, seeking the quick glint of white that marks the rooster's head. The hens, all brown, blended so perfectly with the growth that they were invisible save when in motion.

Lee had always found quail exciting. A reason may have been that they were birds to be hunted. Another reason was perhaps that by their very shrewdness and their will to maintain their species they had withstood man's seasonal efforts to destroy them.

One late afternoon, spring before last, Lee had disturbed a mother quail and her brood near a blackberry patch. She had fluttered up in front of him, whistling softly, and her babies, no larger than a man's thumb, had scuttled in all directions, vanishing almost instantly. In a second the ground in front of him had been alive with swift little streaks, and in the next second all had been still . . . all, that is, except for the mother bird, which was fluttering and flopping a few feet ahead, making a show of being crippled and helpless. Lee had rushed toward her, to pick her up and hold her; and just as he had stooped to seize the poor hurt thing, she had flashed away with a roar of perfectly good wings.

Feeling rather silly over having been tricked, Lee had stood there for a time, watching for some motion in the leaves and grass where the tiny ones had disappeared. He knew they were all around him, but no leaf trembled to betray a hiding-place.

It was things like this that made the quail a sort of special bird, Lee thought.

Sad was down now, crawling. His plumy tail, the barometer of a setter's excitement, whipped back and forth.

"Easy, boy!" Lee called, speaking softly, for he was nearly choked by the excitement of it.

What if Sad came down on a real point his first time out! Lee wished Mr. Tomlin could see the runt now. The old man's bushy brows would really be high and lively with pride.

"Let it be quail!" he whispered.

Then a bird flew up out ahead of the pup, and another and another. But there was no roar of wings; there was just a soft fluttering common to the flight of ordinary birds. And Lee saw a glint of dull yellow on their breasts.

Sad leaped high and lunged after them. He was barking and yipping ecstatically, his black ears laid back and flopping.

"Field larks!" Lee said miserably. "Just ol' field larks." Then he whistled for Sad, but the setter was racing madly after the birds.

In the course of this chase, Sad flushed a rabbit from a briar clump. With a joyous bellow he veered off in wild pursuit of it, and they disappeared over the brow of a small rise.

Lee felt better when his father showed enthusiasm over Sad's interest in the larks. "Just so he hunts something," the man said. "Why, I've had seasoned bird dogs drop to a dead point on field larks."

"Did they run and bark when the birds flew up?" Lee wanted to know. "And did they take out after a rabbit the next minute?"

"I've seen pretty good dogs that couldn't resist running a cottontail now an' then," Mr. Langston told him. "You stop trying to think of Sad as a trained dog. He's just in kindergarten. It takes time to make a good bird dog, time an' patience. Sad'll be a dandy some day." He looked quickly at Mrs. Langston, who had the air of ignoring their conversation.

"We'd better find out whether he's gun-shy or not," Lee said. "That's mighty important."

"You don't need to worry about that," Mrs. Langston put in quickly. "He's not shy about anything else. Besides, it shouldn't matter a lot if he's gun-shy."

The silence was painful. Mr. Langston broke it: "You mean there won't be guns shot over Sad, I guess."

Lee took a deep breath. Here it was again! From the look on his father's face, he knew there could be a showdown, and soon.

"You know as well as I do what I meant." Her face was tight, and she was about to cry. "When the pup was brought here, right at the first, I told you how I felt about the hunting business. I still feel the same way."

"Nell," the man said gently, "maybe you can hold me to a promise I made you a long time ago. I guess you can hold me to it. But Lee's growing up, and you'd be selfish to put the burden of that promise on him, too."

She started to leave the table.

"Wait," he begged. "Hear what I want to say—then cry if you want to."

"I don't want to cry!" she said, speaking the words fast and in a voice that trembled. Her eyes were bright, and she was blinking hard. "Go on. Say what you want to say."

"All right, I will." He leaned forward and knocked his pipe out against the inner jamb of the fireplace. "The best times I had as a boy came in bird hunting, roaming these hills and hollows with a gun and a dog. I never wanted to look for a poolroom or a pinball machine, for being out there in the woods and along the ridges was so much more fun. It had everything. It satisfied something in me that's in every boy—maybe the deep wish in us to outwit nature and get our food from it. In just *hunting* there's a lot of man's history bound up, you know, Nell. There's a lot to it that I can't even put in words; it's too big and exciting and wonderful . . ."

He paused, cleared his throat as if embarrassed by his unusual flight into words. Then he went on: "I learned from my dog, maybe more than he learned from me. Maybe I learned from the owls and the hawks and the quail I hunted, too. And there was always something new and wonderful just over the next rise. It made me a better man, Nell. I know it did." He reached to take her hand. "It made me a good enough man for you to marry. See?" He laughed softly.

"Silly!" she said in a choked voice and gripped his fingers hard.

"Lee has just as much right to such pleasures as I had. He'll be careful with a gun, and I want to get him a new one this fall. Lee's growing up, Nell, and it's time. If he has to wait 'til he's a man on his own, the boy will be gone and he's been cheated out of something he can't go back and get, for it'll be too late then."

"I'm not wanting to cheat him. You know I've no intention of doing that."

"But it amounts to just that. Look, Nell, Lee does a man's work, and I think he deserves a boy's pleasures. He's past the point of slingshots and marbles and throwing green persimmons with a long, sharp stick."

"Oh, I know that! He's past the paper-doll stage, too. But why does he want a gun? Why can't he want something safe, like a—a—well, like a wheelbarrow!"

Mr. Langston laughed, and Lee sensed there was a lightness in his manner, which hinted that they had passed the most difficult point.

"You see how hard it was to think of something to take the place of a gun?" the man asked.

"Well, if Lee has to hunt," she said slowly—and it was plain that she was relieved to have the matter settled—"I want you to go with him. Forget the promise you made me. You've kept it long enough." She left her chair abruptly. "Now you two men find something to do more worthwhile than outmaneuvering the only woman in the house. I still have the supper dishes to wash."

When she had gone from hearing, Mr. Langston said, not triumpantly but as if it were a fact that Lee should remember, "Things usually straighten out when a fellow faces them. You want a sixteen- or a twenty-gauge gun?"

"Let's look at a few, first chance we have," Lee replied. He had tried to keep his voice calm, but it was shaking.

They drove to town on Saturday and went to Hayward's Hardware Store. For thirty minutes they examined shotguns, hefting, aiming comparing one's balance with that of another. They checked on double-barrels, pumps and automatics.

"For a boy of Lee's build and height," the merchant said,

"I'd recommend this sixteen-gauge pump. It's open bore, and I'm sure it puts out a pretty pattern."

"Mind if we take two or three of these guns outside the city limits and try 'em out?" Mr. Langston asked. "Or would that make 'em secondhand?"

"If it did, I wouldn't handle any more like 'em," said Mr. Hayward. "They'd be mighty poor guns to start with. Here, take a few shells and some wrapping paper for targets."

Careful not to scratch the shiny stocks or barrels, Lee and his dad drove to a patch of woods near town and put up a target. After three shots from each gun, using fresh paper after each shot and studying the patterns made from different distances, they settled on the sixteen-gauge pump.

"Does it kick much?" Mr. Langston asked.

"I was so excited," Lee told him, "I couldn't have felt a mule kick."

Back at the store, they bought the sixteen-gauge pump and four boxes of shells with number 8 shot.

"I hear there's a good crop of birds this fall," Mr. Hayward said. "How is it out your way?"

"Fair, I think." Mr. Langston busied himself with writing a check. "This'll be the first season in years that I've done any bird-hunting."

"How about selling you a gun?"

"I've still got that old double-barrel my daddy used when he and Mr. Tomlin hunted together. It'll reach out and get 'em."

"I know that old double. They don't make guns like that any more." The merchant blotted the check carefully. "By the way, Guy Tomlin was in here this morning. He says his daddy's ailing."

"That so? We'll have to go out and see the old fellow, Lee."

"I feel sorry for Mr. Luke Tomlin," Mr. Hayward declared. "Things turned out mighty poorly for him."

"What's Guy doing here?" Mr. Langston asked.

"He didn't say. Maybe he came out to see about his father —or to wheedle him out of some more money."

Before leaving for home, Lee and his father went to a grocery store for week-end extras. They bought also some large firecrackers to use in acquainting Sad with sudden explosions. "Cheaper than gunshells," Mr. Langston pointed out.

Riding home, Lee held his new gun as tenderly as if it were a rare piece of Venetian glass, stroking it occasionally.

"Take care of it," Mr. Langston said, "and it'll last you a lifetime."

"I'll keep it as new as grease and love can do the job," Lee promised.

In sight of the house, they noticed a car parked in front of the yard. Drawing nearer, they saw that it bore an out-of-state license, and that a heavy-set man was at the wheel.

"Whatever he's selling," Mr. Langston said dryly, "we're not buying." He swung into the driveway.

The man slid from his car and called affably, "Well, Hurd, how are you? Long time, no see, fella." He advanced with outstretched hand.

Lee thought there was something familiar in the stranger's face, which was flushed as if from a tight collar. He wore a blue bow tie. His brown suit was very close-fitting and shiny at stress points.

"Well, it's Guy Tomlin!" Mr. Langston said. "It *has* been a long time, Guy. What're you doing these days?"

"Well, I've been doin' some paint contractin' in Memphis," the visitor told him, "but I'm fixin' to git back in the dog business. Hi, young fella," he greeted Lee. "Quite a popgun you've got there."

"Yes, sir." Lee knew instantly that he disliked the man, whom he had seen only once before, two or three years ago. He started on toward the house to show his mother the new gun, but Guy Tomlin's next words stopped him cold. He turned to listen.

"Drove over to talk with you about the dog, Hurd," the man was saying pleasantly. He nodded toward the pen, where Sad was barking a loud greeting to Lee.

"What about the dog?" Mr. Langston asked.

"Well, you see, it's like this. An' I want you to understand how I feel about it, Hurd, so there'll be no hard feelin's. Bein's as you an' me was just about raised up together, I figure—"

"What're you beating about the bush for?" Mr. Langston interrupted.

"Well, Hurd, Pa's gettin' pretty old, an' he's bullheaded. You know how old folks get sometimes, when they think the young ones oughta stayed out in the sticks an' scrambled for a few dollars a year. As you know, Pa got sore when Mary Lou run off with that Embry Wales, like she did. Sure, he was disappointed, an' all that—"

"You started off talking about the dog," Mr. Langston cut in. "What does he have to do with what you're talking about now?"

"Now, Hurd, I just wanted you to have the full story so you'd understand. Fam'ly business gets mighty complicated at times, you know." He paused, ran a thick forefinger for a distance between neck and tight collar. "What I'm gettin' at is that the dog Pa give your boy was mine. That's how it is."

Lee felt a cold chill, then a hot wave chasing it up and down his spine. He was gripping his new gun very hard, but not aware of it.

"Is that so?" Mr. Langston inquired slowly, eyes fixed steadily on the face of Guy Tomlin. "Mr. Tomlin didn't say a word about that back in April, when he gave Lee the pup. Had he offered you the runt of the litter?"

"Well, no, not the runt. I was s'posed to get the pick of the males of that litter. That's how it was. 'Course, as it come out, the dog you've got was the only male of the litter, so he's mine."

Mr. Langston nodded, thinking about it. The time seemed very long to Lee. His father's easy manner frightened him.

"We wouldn't have accepted the pup," Mr. Langston said at last, still speaking pleasantly, "if we'd known it was yours, Guy. 'Course, we took him and raised him, and we've worried with him an awful lot. Now, right on the edge of the bird season, would be a bad time for Lee to give him up. He likes the dog pretty much."

"Sure, a kid likes a dog." Guy Tomlin's voice had risen a tone or two, and his face was a deeper red. "The old man oughtn't to've give him away." He shrugged, then added apologetically, "But he's slippin', you know. His mind's not as sharp as—"

"It's as sharp as any old man's mind ought to be," Mr. Langston said shortly.

"I figured you wouldn't see it like I do," Guy Tomlin said with an air of understanding. "I've knowed the old man better than you have, an' I can tell how he's slippin' up here." He tapped his temple with a thick forefinger. "He forgets things, an' he imagines things, too. Pa's gettin' along toward eighty, you know. As for the dog, I'll be glad to pay you for the trouble you've went to account of him, long as it's a reasonable charge, I mean."

"I don't think we'll give up the dog," Mr. Langston said, speaking almost gently. "As for paying for the trouble we've all been to because of the pup, you don't have that much money. You couldn't even borrow enough. We're just not in the market, Guy."

"Now, I didn't come here to raise a ruckus, Hurd, but when a man takes my proppity an' won't give it up—"

"Go get your dad," Mr. Langston broke in. "If he comes here and tells Lee it's your dog, then we'll talk business."

"I don't need the ol' crank!" Guy Tomlin snapped. "I'll get the sheriff, that's who I'll get." He shook an angry forefinger at Lee. "An' when I tell him your boy stood there with a shotgun while I tried to persuade you to do the right thing, somebody'll be in deep trouble! I'll gar'ntee that!"

Hurd Langston laughed. "You go get Jim Taylor," he invited. "We'll be here, gun and all, when you come back with him."

5

As lee watched guy tomlin's car disappear in angry haste down the highway, his face was white, and there was a weak feeling deep within him. He had never foreseen a threat like this. That anyone else had the remotest claim on Sad, or even pretended to have a claim on him, had never occurred to Lee Langston.

"S'pose he'll go for the sheriff?" Lee asked, waiting for his father to join him at the steps.

Mr. Langston's face was tight, and the anger he had held back was showing through. "I think he was bluffing. Guy's the kind who'll bulldoze the other fellow as far as he can."

"I thought for a minute he'd jump you. His face was red as a turkey snout."

"I wasn't worried about Guy jumping me." Mr. Langston laughed shortly. "I've known him for a long time." Then he chuckled. "Besides, you were standing there with a brand-new gun."

Lee laughed nervously. "*Does* sound bad," he admitted.

Mrs. Langston, her blue eyes angry, met them at the front door. "He wanted me to let him have Sad before you all came home. After all the misery we've gone through with that dog, he comes here out of a blue sky, claiming him! That's brass!"

74

"That's Guy's style," Mr. Langston told her. "He's always been a bully an' a sharpie. Say, look at Lee's new gun. It's a beauty."

"If a gun can be pretty," she said, "it is."

Mr. Langston phoned the office of Sheriff Jim Taylor. When he had finished with the chief county official, he looked pleased. "Guy Tomlin's there right now," he told Lee and Mrs. Langston.

"Swearing out a warrant for you?" she asked. "What makes you look so happy about that?"

"No, he got picked up for speeding on his way to town. He's trying to outtalk Jim now and persuade him to drop the matter."

"Well, good!" she exclaimed. "That's real justice, I think."

"And Jim told me something else interesting," Mr. Langston informed her. "He's heard that Joe Ray is figuring on running for sheriff next spring."

"Why is that so interesting?" she wanted to know.

"Well, Joe'll need all the votes he can get. If he goes ahead on this Winston deal an' sells hunting rights on his land, he'll lose a lot of votes. See?"

"How you men do try to outfigure each other!" she said with appreciation. "I'd never have thought of that."

"You're not a man," he reminded her. "By the way, you and Lee ought to drive over this afternoon and see how old man Tomlin is. I'll stick around, in case Guy Tomlin shows up again."

"Let's go out right now," Lee suggested, "and shoot off some of the firecrackers. I'm just wonderin' how Sad'll act."

"And I'll bake a cake for Mr. Tomlin," said Mrs. Langston. "It won't take long."

Lee and his dad went out toward the dog pen. At sight of them Sad raced and whirled about the enclosure, then barked pleadingly when they stopped several yards away.

Lee fired a fuse and tossed the 'cracker to a safe distance and toward the pen. It exploded with about the volume and shock of a twenty-gauge shell.

Sad dropped as if clubbed, then scrambled up and lunged for the safety of the little house, disappearing into it.

Lee called and whistled him out again. He came forth warily, his tail tucked.

"Dogs have sensitive ears," Mr. Langston said. " 'Specially high-strung dogs like Sad. Sharp noises hurt. We'd better back up to shoot the next firecracker."

The second explosion occurred a few yards farther back from the pen. This time, the setter merely shivered a little. He was standing still, studying the noisemakers quizzically. His head was high, ears cocked sharply forward, brow deeply wrinkled. His attitude was one of alertness and puzzlement, as if he could not quite decide what was wrong with two heretofore rather dependable people. Why they were now acting so strangely, making such shocking noises, was entirely beyond him to reason out.

For the third firecracker they moved a little nearer to the pen. This time, Sad barked and thrashed his tail as if he had suddenly decided to accept the whole thing as a game. Yes, he would go along with them, and if they were happy over it, so was he.

"I don't think we need to worry about gun-shyness," Mr. Langston said. "We'll shoot some more of these in a day or two, then we'll try the shotgun."

When Lee and his mother arrived at the Tomlin place at

shortly after three that afternoon, they found the old man alone, sitting in front of his fireplace. He was heavily dressed, wearing a thick woolen muffler about his neck. It was very warm in the room. His old four-poster bed, made of intricately carved walnut, was badly tousled, long unmade.

"I reckin' it's the flu," the old man said hoarsely. "That, or I'm about wore out."

"Oh, you'll be all right," Mrs. Langston assured him. "You just shouldn't be living by yourself this way. I think your main trouble is being lonesome."

"Not lonesome," he said shortly. "Besides, I get a lot of time for thinkin' an' rememberin' how it was back years ago, when life was worth livin'. What's in that box you brought?"

"I made you a cake. There are some fresh eggs in the box, too, and a pone of old-fashioned salt-rising bread. Just some odds and ends." She took off her coat. "Whether you like it or not, I'm going to make your bed and straighten up this room a little."

"Now, don't you bother—" he began. "Please do, Miss Nell. What this ol' house needs is a woman's touch, if a house ever did! But I'm ashamed you come here when everything was so tore up like this."

"Where do you keep your fresh sheets?" she asked, ignoring his apology.

"There're some washed ones in that chest by the window," he told her. "I don't iron my sheets any more. They won't have no more wrinkles than I have, anyway."

"I'll iron a pair for you." She caught up two long-unused flatirons lying at the end of the hearth and set them to heat in front of bright coals she raked out. "Mary Lou and Embry ought to be out here with you, taking care of things like this. That's what I think, even if you—"

"You're too nice to fuss with," he said gently. "You know I've got no time for that Embry Wales."

"Now, Mr. Tomlin, you're just cutting off your nose to spite your face." Mrs. Langston could say such things, which needed saying, better than anyone else, she was sure. "I don't sorrow and wishing and a deep loneliness that had only one want to fuss, either, but I'm getting in touch with Mary Lou as soon as I can, whether it's meddling or not. She has a right to know how things are with you, no matter what you say about it."

"Why should she care?" His voice was a little trembly. "She's got what she wanted, worthless as it is!"

Lee could see the old fellow's face working, and he sensed that behind the expression of stubborn anger there were cure.

"Now, what's the matter with Embry?" Mrs. Langston scolded, busy with dusting the old marble-topped dresser.

"He's a Wales—second-rate folks. That's enough, ain't it?"

"But he's *first*-rate with Mary Lou. That should be enough for you, seems to me. Long as she's satisfied—"

"What did the Waleses ever do?" the old man asked as if that should clinch the matter for good and all. "Tell me one good thing the Waleses ever did for themselves or for anybody else."

"Oh, I know Embry's father came in here and tried to outdo you as a dog trainer," Mrs. Langston admitted. "And I know he could never beat you at the game, for you were a master trainer if one ever lived. But you shouldn't hold that against him."

"I licked him every time!" Mr. Tomlin recalled with grim pleasure. "As for that Embry, what has he ever done worthwhile? He fooled aroun' with dogs an' hot-rod cars an'—"

"But he was never in trouble," Mrs. Langston interrupted. "I never heard one really bad thing about Embry."

"It's a wonder he didn't get in trouble, though. He had all the talents for it." Then he snorted explosively. "Mary Lou had everything she needed right here. It should've been everything she wanted, too. She knew it'd be her place some day. On top of all that, she up an' run off with—"

"She didn't have everything she needed," Mrs. Langston interrupted sharply. "A grandpa can't take the place of somebody one's own age. You ought to know that. But we're about to work up an argument that won't do any good at all. The simple truth is that you need Mary Lou now, and I'm going to see that she comes out here for a while, even if you won't let Embry come."

"He won't want to come," Mr. Tomlin said with confidence. "I told him right after he sneaked out here an' stole Mary Lou never to set foot on this place again."

"He's no more to blame for the elopement than she was. It takes two, Mr. Tomlin. The truth is, I don't think you were honest or fair when you ordered Embry to stay away from here. That was a much worse thing than he did. In fact, I think he showed good sense when he fell in love with Mary Lou."

Mr. Tomlin said nothing for a time. He was looking at the changing patterns of light deep in the bed of bright coals of the fireplace.

Mrs. Langston was scrubbing a windowpane vigorously, each motion sending out a plaintive squeak. "I don't want

to make you feel bad," she said at last, "but defending a
mistake is worse than making it sometimes. You ought to
forget how you felt about Embry a year ago and—"

"I guess I'm too hardheaded for that," he broke in, speaking without anger. "Too downright hardheaded!" Then he
turned to Lee and asked, "How's that pup comin' along?"

"Full of the dickens," Lee told him, "and still growin' fast.
By the way, he nearly came down on point not long ago—on
field larks."

"That's good. Wish I'd been there. Boy, I'd love to shoot
over a good dog again. But that time's gone."

"Maybe not. Look, when I get some coveys spotted near
the field roads, I'll come and get you and we'll hunt from the
pickup. When Sad points, we'll get out and—"

"Sounds nice an' easy," Mr. Tomlin said, "but even that'd
be hard on my old bones."

After a pause, during which Lee tried hard to think of a
smooth way to bring up an unpleasant matter, he said, "Mr.
Guy Tomlin was at our house this morning."

"That so?" the old man asked quickly. "He came by here
for a little while last night, an' I told him not to bother you
all about that pup."

"He didn't bother us a lot," Lee said. "Dad just told him
he couldn't have Sad."

"I'm sorry he pestered you." Mr. Tomlin rocked slowly for
a moment, then added, "He'd just sell the pup to somebody.
Guy's too lazy to hunt." Then he got up stiffly from the
rocker and moved to the battered old desk between his bed
and the north window. He picked up a sheet of ruled paper
and came back to his rocker. "This here is proof of your
ownership. I wrote it out last night, after Guy had gone.
Figured on mailin' it to you."

"Guy didn't even spend the night here?" Mrs. Langston asked.

"He didn't. Says it's too quiet out here in the sticks." Then, to Lee, "Read what I wrote."

Slowly and with effort he hoped was not obvious, Lee deciphered the wavery, old-fashioned handwriting: *I gave Lee Langston the Tomlin setter, Black Saddle, which he calls Sad. Nobody else has a claim on the dog. Anybody that says he has is a liar.* The paper was signed *Luke Tomlin* in a firm, clear hand, and beneath the signature was the date.

"This ought to clear things up," Lee said. "Much obliged."

"Not 't'all." The old man coughed. " 'Course, if somebody proves I wasn't sound of mind when I wrote it, that's somethin' else."

"What a silly notion!" Mrs. Langston cried, turning from the bed, which she was making ready for the fresh sheets. "Who on earth would say such a—?"

"Guy said last night that I ought to go an' live where there are other people my age an' be cared for by the state. He could've meant the asylum, you know."

"But surely he didn't."

"Guy's my only son now, even if he is adopted. If he could get me put away somewhere an' be appointed administrator of what little I have—well, he'd be better off than he is now. Such things do happen to old people, you know."

"Well, it won't happen to you," Mrs. Langston promised with feeling. "Don't you worry a minute about it, either."

The room had been cleaned by now, and the bed improved with fresh, ironed sheets. Mrs. Langston had sneaked enough fresh air into the room to relieve it somewhat of the mingled odors of stale pipe tobacco and soiled clothes. It was time to go home.

"You're awful nice," Mr. Tomlin said, leaving his rocker. "I wish I had a daughter like you."

"You've a granddaughter just as nice," Mrs. Langston reminded him. "No, don't you say a word, now. We've already fussed enough. Just take care of yourself; and if anybody makes a move to send you off *any*where, you just let us know. And be careful not to eat too much of that cake. It may be a little heavy."

"It won't be heavy enough to be a burden," he said dryly. "I thank you so much, Miss Nell."

On their way home Lee and his mother stopped in town, where Mrs. Langston made inquiries concerning the Memphis address of Mary Lou Tomlin Wales. Then she placed a telephone call. Lee was near enough to the booth to hear her talking with Mary Lou:

"It doesn't matter whether Embry goes out there with you or not; you go and see after that old man. He's your grandfather, and you have a duty to him right now—Embry?—Oh, he's young; he can take care of himself."

Mary Lou must have protested, for Mrs. Langston's next words were sharply spoken: "It doesn't matter what he thinks of Embry . . . not right now, anyway. And Mr. Tomlin's old enough to have a right to his own opinions, even some wrong ones. What? Embry has a lot of pride? Well, so has your grandpa, and his pride is a lot older than Embry's."

And after a brief pause Mrs. Langston said, "Well, you'll have to decide what to do, but if you don't want to be ashamed of yourself the rest of your life, you'd better get out there and take care of that poor old fellow. Good-bye."

When they were headed homeward from town, Mrs. Langston said abruptly, "Lee, I'm an awful meddler." A half mile farther on she said, "That low-down Guy Tomlin!"

Lee fished the ruled paper from his pocket, handed it to her. "This ought to clear things up pretty well. Looks as if all the Tomlins, even includin' the dogs, have pretty strong feelin's."

At home, they found Mr. Langston working with Sad on retrieving, playing the endless pitch-out-bring-back game. No one had been there during the afternoon, and no word had come from Guy Tomlin.

"You s'pose he'd try to steal Sad?" Lee wondered.

"I wouldn't put it past him," Mr. Langston said. "We'll leave the back-yard light on for a few nights. That, along with Sad's barking when anybody comes around his pen, ought to discourage a thief."

Two afternoons following school the next week, Lee and Sad took brief excursions along the ridge southwest of the house. He left his gun at home, for bird season was not yet open, but he was sorely tempted to carry it just for the feel of it on his shoulder and for the thrill of sliding his hand along the cool, blued barrel, and for the feel of the shiny, varnished stock. He longed to swing along behind Sad, gun barrel cradled in left arm, pretending to be on the alert for scattered quail that might roar up at any second from hastily chosen coverts.

Only a few days stood between him and the pleasures he must now imagine, for Monday, the tenth of November, would be opening day.

Sad raced and lunged through the sedge, snorting and snuffling. Again, as on that first afternoon round, he came almost to point on larks. He dropped low, head and back making a straight line, tail almost stiff . . . then the larks flew up, one here, two there, and he raced after them, bellowing joyously.

On the second afternoon, just at sunset, Sad struck a scent that brought him suddenly to a crawl in a tangle of briars and sumac.

"Easy, boy!" Lee begged. "Easy, now!"

Reaching a more open stretch, Sad stood up cautiously, but he was still creeping. Now he was almost on point, and just the end of his long-feathered tail was in motion.

Lee had moved around the thicket. "Whoa!" he called in a voice that was scarcely more than a croak. His heart was pounding hard, nearly choking him. "Whoa, boy!" This *must* be quail! At no other time had Sad been quite so thoroughly controlled from tip to tip by a scent. Now it was as if an ecstasy of some marvelous kind had caught him in its grip; as if some miracle, invisible and unaccountable, had moved into him from the earth and the air, catching him in a spell for which he had unknowingly waited.

It was a marvelous sight. Lee Langston stood there, tense, hoping, quivering throughout with the joy of it. The picture of Sad on his first point was etched hard and sharp on the boy's mind. It was a dream come true, a long-held hope realized.

No, he was not quite on point. He was creeping ahead so smoothly and so slowly he seemed to be flowing. He was crouched so that Lee could not see his legs clearly, and it was only by the changing relation of dog and surrounding growth that Lee could be sure that he was moving.

Now Sad was dead still. The end of his tail was motionless now, and his whole body was locked in that mysterious stance known simply as "point."

Lee's mouth and throat were dry, for breath was coming hot and fast. Wide-eyed, he watched the dog held there like stone by what man calls "instinct." In a vague sort of way, Lee knew that generations of great hunters had focused into that marvelous moment and that the last Tomlin was held paralyzed in the grip of his own heritage. This was something that time and blood had built into him, something out of the rich, dim past.

Lee ached with the strain of it. He knew, somehow, that field larks had not caused this; nor was it a wily rabbit. It was quail this time. Sad would not freeze like this on anything but quail. . . .

Then it was over. It had seemed a far longer time than the few seconds it had actually lasted. Sad lunged forward with a wild yelp, and the covey burst up with a roar of wings like light thunder. Brown rockets they were, shooting off into the cool sunset air, each to its own direction, and with no confusion, for quail huddle in a circle, heads out, tails in, so that when sudden flight is necessary they will not plummet into each other.

"Sad!" Lee cried, for the setter was leaping and bellowing after the birds. "Sad!" He ran after the dog, unmindful of briars and growth that raked him in his happy haste.

When he finally caught the pup, Lee hugged him. "You did it!" he cried happily, saying it over and over. "You did it! You pointed quail! That's the way, boy!" And, careless of the hot, red tongue raking across his face, he hugged Sad close, and they rolled on the cool, dampening ground.

Sad finally leaped away, ran a swift circle, barking with every lunge. He seemed to be saying, "What a dog am I! And I can do it again! Come!"

Lee got up. Off to the northwest, he could see the last two birds of the scattered covey sailing low just above the sedge, dropping toward a thicket of head-high pines. It would be almost black-dark before they could follow the singles and try for another point and then get back to the house. The sun was down, leaving the west a soft red, with slivers of slate-colored cloud lying horizontally along the horizon just above the trees that fringed the ridge top in that direction.

"Let's go home," he said happily. "Let's go home and tell about it."

They ran most of the way, both boy and dog filled with a sense of happy accomplishment. Lee could hardly wait to see his father's face when he told him of Sad's point—the trailing, the barely perceptible motion just before the point, the rigid statue, with every muscle still, Sad had made when he was down on the birds.

"And he held the birds—it seemed like an hour—before he broke point and leaped in on 'em. . . ."

He worked out the telling, so that it would be most effective. He wondered how much his mother would enjoy the account, since it would be a forecast of time to come, of hunts to come.

It was nearly dark when Lee went through the back gate, having turned Sad into the pen. His father was waiting on the back porch.

"He found quail!" Lee cried. "He came down on point and held for—"

"Well, now!" Mr. Langston interruped gladly. "Seems we've got a real bird dog on our hands, doesn't it?"

" 'Course, he ran after the birds, barkin' and leapin'," Lee added.

"That's all right. Sad's just a pup. Keep remembering that."

At supper that evening Lee said with dour generosity,

"When the season opens Monday, you needn't sit around here, wishin', just because I need educatin'."

The phone rang then. Lee could tell that it was Mary Lou and that she had gone out to stay indefinitely with Mr. Tomlin.

"I'm so glad he's better," Mrs. Langston said. "You take care of him, now, and if you need me, call me."

When she had hung up, Lee said, "Well, your meddlin' paid off."

"It does, sometimes. And she said that Embry has a job in Riptonville now, so he can be near by."

On Monday morning, seeing how miserable Lee was over having to go to school, Mr. Langston said, "I won't make a move toward bird hunting before Saturday, when you can go, too. Don't be so long-faced."

"Oh, Dad, go on and hunt birds!" Lee was trying hard to be unselfish about the business. "Just because—"

"Well," Mr. Langston broke in dryly, "I don't have a dog. You see—"

"I might lend you mine," Lee said, trying to match his mood. "Of course, he's young, but—"

It was very hard on Lee to have to go to school on Monday morning. Even in town and with schoolroom windows closed, he fancied he heard guns, and he had to fight hard to keep his mind occupied with academic matters. But all the while he saw, back in his unhappy imagination, tireless setters and pointers racing through the soft sedge which laid a golden tan over the valleys and ridges, saw them frozen on point, waiting for their masters to come up and flush their finds. The week dragged slowly by.

The days were growing shorter and shorter, so that after

Lee had reached home from school, there was too little day-light left for a hunt.

But Saturday came at last, bright and clear. Lee was up at dawn. He fed Sad early, aware that a dog should not hunt soon after eating. There had been a light frost during the night, and thin ice made a bright sheet in Sad's watering pan. The day would be perfect for hunting.

After breakfast, Mrs. Langston packed a lunch for the hunters. She went about it quietly, perhaps a little grimly, Lee thought, but he knew how she must feel. This was a thing she had never expected to do. Until quite lately, she had been free from fear of guns in connection with her loved ones, but now she was taking part in the very plans she had been determined to deny.

Lee wished she could share his happiness. He wanted to say, "Don't you worry about us; we'll be careful," but he was afraid to say anything. If she started crying, neither he nor his dad would have the heart to leave her there. Of course, she seldom cried about things, and he knew that she was not the kind to back down from a clear agreement. He knew that a mother like her would not deny her son the right to grow up and go on toward being a man. She knew that he was past the time of playing with toys, of making whistles and popguns and little, thin-whittled wooden whizzers to whirl about his head on a string, just for the sound they made.

Lee noted how tactfully his father talked this morning, how cheerfully—at the risk of being obvious, Lee feared—he said, "Nell, why don't you go to town and buy you a new dress? You haven't had a new dress in a year or two, have you?"

"I bought two last spring, at Haralson's sale," she told him. "I don't need a new dress as much as you need a new suit."

"Oh, I look about the same, no matter what I wear." Then, very optimistically, he said, "Better have some hot grease ready when we get back here. We'll have some birds, I'll guarantee you."

"And I'll have rice ready for the browned gravy," she promised.

Lee knew that neither of them was really thinking about clothes or what would be served for supper. They talked like that to hide the real matter between them. Often he had sensed this when their words had been so different from their true thoughts. He wondered if all mothers and fathers beat around bushes that bristled with hidden thorns.

An hour after breakfast, but still early for beginning the hunt, Lee and his father, with Sad in the bed of the pickup, drove off. Mrs. Langston watched from the back porch. Sad barked back at her until they had rounded the bend of the road leading toward the ridge cupping the creek bottom.

Frost was still on the shaded grass. The dry smell of fall, fragrant with woodsmoke from distant chimneys, was on the air. They followed along the ridge for three miles, then parked in a good turn-around place. Lee untied Sad.

Yelping with delight, the setter leaped from the pickup and raced forth into the tall sedge.

"Birds hold close on cold mornings," Mr. Langston said. "They don't get out and feed much, leaving trails, 'til things warm up."

The crack of a gun sounded in the distance, on the far side of the ridge.

"We're not the first ones out, anyway," Lee said. "Look, Sad's on a trail already."

"He'll move like that a lot, 'til he learns better." Mr.

Langston laughed a little. "Your school's out today; Sad's is just beginning."

They followed the setter along the west side of the ridge. Other shots sounded off there, nearer each time.

"I hoped we wouldn't have company," Mr. Langston said. "My Gordon and I used to hunt along here, years ago. Once I found ten coveys between here and that clump of pines off to the west, yonder."

Sad disappeared over the brow of the ridge, ignoring Lee's call to slow down. He would be, it was clear, a wide ranger, perhaps too wide at first.

"Let him go," Mr. Langston said. "He'll have to learn by experience. Right now, he hasn't the least idea why you're whistling and yelling at him."

Following the bounding setter, they topped the rise. As far as they could see, there were sedge hills and pines stretching on and on to the pale horizon.

Two pointers were ranging far off down there, a little this side of the foot of the slope. Sad was heading straight for them.

"Come on," Mr. Langston said, walking faster. "See if you can call him back."

Lee whistled and yelled, but Sad paid no attention. Now he was barking at the pointers and making for them in great, happy bounds.

The larger of the two dogs, a black-and-white "rip-rap," dropped on point. A man with his gun at ready came around a fringe of growth and called, "Hold it, Jim! Hold, *boy!*"

The other dog, a liver-and-white, fell on point behind Jim, "backing," or honoring, the find.

"Sad!" Mr. Langston bellowed. "You, Sad!"

But the setter leaped joyously onward. He knew nothing of the finer points of field etiquette. All he could see now was new friends to be met. For a long time he had been penned up, and now he was free.

When Sad was fifteen feet from the pointers, in front and to the left of the still "rip-rap," the covey roared up from a clump of sedge between them. As if it had been planned, they whipped to the right and veered off toward the rim of the woods down the slope.

Sad leaped high in shock, then raced after the birds. As he ran, he yipped in frenzied joy.

"Hey, *you!*" yelled the man with the gun down there, obviously angered by this development. "Git 'im, Jim!"

The big pointer was already going after Sad. Lee could hear him growling as he lunged in the wake of the impudent, ill-mannered setter.

"*Sad!*" Lee cried. "Here, *Sad!*"

The Llewellyn stopped and looked back, perhaps not so much in obedience as in frustration, for he realized that the birds had a decided advantage over him. Already they had disappeared among the pines off there.

The big pointer lunged for him and knocked him end over end. Then he was on the startled setter, snapping and slashing. Sad yelped and struggled desperately for freedom, but the attacker was old and fieldwise. He was maneuvering for a hold on the setter's throat.

"Stop the fight!" Mr. Langston called to the man. "Call off your pointer. Our dog's just a pup."

"You better keep 'im at home, then," the man answered as he walked on toward the struggling, snapping pair.

The "rip-rap" was bigger and stronger than Sad, and this

was clearly not his first fight. Whether he had attacked because the setter had spoiled his find was hard to tell, for seasoned bird dogs have been known to thrash young upstarts for just such errors. Whatever his reason for the assault, the big pointer was on top of the scrambling, yowling pup and giving him a terrific going-over.

Lee was outrunning his dad. He caught up a dead stick and brandished it, crying, "Stop the fight! Stop it!"

"Don't you hit that pointer, boy," the man ordered. He was coming faster now. "That's a field-trial dog. Don't you—"

"Call 'im off, then," Lee said hotly. "My pup's never had a fight in his life."

But Sad, in his wild desperation, made it unnecessary to call off the pointer. He was busy in his own behalf, and he had the advantage of speed and of an inspiring fear. The first few seconds of the fight had found him startled, off balance and obsessed with the worthy idea of getting loose. Seeing how difficult that was, he had resourcefully sought another solution; in brief, he had clamped down on the pointer's left foreleg, driving his sharpest teeth into muscle and bone. At the same time he had made a wild lunge to the left and dumped the attacker heavily on his side.

The "rip-rap" roared in surprised rage and slashed at the pup's ear, drawing blood.

Swiftly Sad released the tortured foreleg of his attacker and leaped away. But he did not run. Another department of instinct had risen to the surface: the Tomlins were fighters as well as hunters. Growling, teeth bared, he leaped for the larger dog, which was now scrambling to his feet, and knocked him down again. Then Sad fell upon the upset

"Git 'im off'n my dog!" the man yelled

pointer, bellowing in righteous rage, ripping and tearing at his throat as if intent on murder itself.

"Git 'im off'n my dog!" the man yelled. "*Stop* 'im!"

Lee darted in and caught Sad's collar. The eager, maddened pup almost snatched him down as he lunged to the attack again.

Now the "rip-rap," roaring with rage, hackles bristled, was on his feet. He was growling and snarling as he dropped to a crouch, ready to leap again to the attack. Then, seeing Lee with raised club, he stopped. His teeth were bared, and he was snarling a warning.

The man moved in and caught the pointer's collar. "Jim!" he snapped. "Easy, fella."

Mr. Langston came up then. "I'm sorry our pup flushed your covey," he said, "but—"

"I see he's just a pup," the man broke in. "I reckin I oughtn't to've sicked Jim on him. He's a Tomlin dog, ain't he?"

"He's the last of the Tomlin line," Lee told the stranger. "This is his first day to hunt. Our name is Langston."

"Pleastermeetcha. I'm Flem Branch, from down nigh Wadley. Trainin' a few dogs this season." He looked at Sad appreciatively. "If you decide to sell that dog, I'll take 'im off'n your hands."

"I raised him from a pup," Lee said simply, as if that were the full answer. "We tried to call him back when he started toward your dogs, but—"

"Sure, he's a pup. I can see that now." Mr. Branch had dropped into a very affable air. "He looks a lot like the last dog I seen with ol' man Luke at the Great Southern Trials. Same markin's an' the same build. They're a fine set of dogs, them Tomlins."

"We figure he'll make a fine dog," Mr. Langston put in. "But dogs are a lot like people; it takes patience and training and a lot of waiting and suffering to bring a pup to a finished field dog."

"Don't I know that!" Mr. Branch agreed with feeling. "An' sometimes, after all a feller's mis'ry, a dog turns out a flop! That's how it goes, all right."

Before they separated, Mr. Langston said, "We'll hunt on the other side of the ridge. That way, the pup shouldn't break up any more points for you."

As they started back up the rise, Lee said, "Ol' Jim's limpin' a little. Looks like Sad did a good job takin' care of himself."

Mr. Langston chuckled. "Next time, maybe the 'rip-rap' won't be so anxious to teach strangers a lesson. Sad's going to be a fighter when it's forced on him. He's too good-natured to pick a fight."

"That was the first time I ever saw him mad," Lee said. "Man, he was boilin'! He might've licked that pointer if they hadn't been separated."

"I doubt that, but maybe he learned to be wary of a dog on point."

ᴥ 6 ᴧ

Before they were halfway down the slope on their side of the ridge, they heard Mr. Branch's gun. He was already among the singles of the covey Sad had flushed.

"One of the pointers over there must be a good singles dog," Mr. Langston said. "A dog's usually better on coveys or singles, and you don't often get one that good on both. A fellow needs two dogs to be fixed up right for bird-hunting, one to range wide and find coveys, the other to hunt close and find the scattered singles."

"Which one's better at retrievin'?" Lee asked.

"The singles dog, usually."

"Sad'll be both," Lee predicted with confidence.

"Possible, all right, but not likely. Right now, from the way he moves out in that long lope of his, I'd say he'll be a covey dog. And that's all right, too. Before you can find singles, which give you the best shooting and really put the birds in your hunting coat, you've got to find coveys."

At the sound of the Branch gun, Sad had stopped, head high as if listening. Perhaps he was trying to relate the sharp reports with the two dogs over there, or perhaps even with the birds he had so impolitely flushed ahead of the "rip-rap."

After standing very still for a moment as if trying to reason something out, he bounded away, head still high, the white of his coat flashing and disappearing according to the height and heaviness of the grass.

"See how he moves into what little wind there is most of the time," Mr. Langston observed. "That's pretty smart for a pup."

"Maybe instinct tells him what to do about the wind," Lee suggested.

His father nodded. "A good dog can catch a wind-borne quail scent and follow it right to a dead point."

"Look at Sad now," Lee said proudly, pointing. "He smells birds, I'll just bet!"

The setter was moving in a stiff-legged trot, head well up, tail whipping from side to side.

"Looks as if he *thinks* he smells 'em, anyway," Mr. Langston agreed. "That's the way he'll move when he winds a covey. His form's mighty pretty."

At the next report from the Branch automatic, Sad stopped again, but for only an instant. His head was still high, cocked inquisitively to one side, right foot raised a little and folded back. Then he went on in his springy, stiff-legged trot and disappeared among the pines.

The hunters moved a little faster now. Mr. Langston said, "One of the finest parts of bird-hunting is watching your dog work. It's not just killing birds; it's really that dog out there, doing something that not even the smartest man on earth can do. He's proving there's a miracle in his nose, and he's working his head off to find what he was born to find."

"Another fine thing about huntin'," Lee added, "is the understandin' that grows up between a dog and its master. They sort of learn to work together, each knowin' what's expected of him."

"You said it well." Mr. Langston laughed softly. "I used to know a fellow who had a female pointer, a slim, black-an'-white-speckled, keen-nosed little beauty that would actually pout if he didn't knock down at least one bird on each covey rise."

"She expected him to do his part, I guess," Lee said.

"Why, in her late years, she got so uppity about it she'd even leave the field and go right back home if he missed two or three shots one after the other. Real prima donna, I guess you'd call her."

Now Sad was acting just as he had acted on the late afternoon when he had pointed the covey in the sumac thicket. He was in a deep crouch, almost crawling, moving slowly.

They hurried. Lee called, "Easy, boy! Careful, Sad!"

By the time they had covered half the distance separating them from the dog, he was barely creeping. His tail was almost still now, straight out behind him, the tip curved slightly upward.

"He'll be a beauty on point!" Mr. Langston said in a voice near whispering. "He's got real form—field-trial form, boy!"

"Reckon we'll ever enter him in one of the big trials?" Lee asked excitedly.

"Never can tell about that. Years ago, old man Tomlin took a lot of big cash prizes at trials, with dogs that looked pretty much like Sad."

"He's got 'em!" Lee stage-whispered. "Careful, *Sad!*"

For a brief moment the setter was perfectly still. Then, after a second or two, he moved on with the ease and silence of a ghost.

"Be ready, now," Mr. Langston said, "but don't throw off the safety 'til the birds come up. Never while walking. That's right—gun barrel pointing up—an' when they rise, pick out one bird instead of blasting into the whole covey." Then he added, to ease Lee's tenseness. "This might be no more'n a little old brown grassbird. They fool seasoned dogs sometimes."

Now Sad was frozen dead-still again, immobile.

"Seems he's made up his mind this time," Mr. Langston said softly. "He's really got whatever it is."

Lee swallowed hard. His mouth was dry, and a hot, tight feeling had welled into his chest. Let it be quail! He was nigh bursting with pride and at the same time as taut as a fiddlestring. His palms were moist against barrel and stock of the new gun. His heart was pounding hard, and he was breathing fast and shallow.

"Hold it!" he begged in a voice that came out in a kind of pleading croak.

They were ten feet from Sad when he leaped—just as he had leaped that other time.

The covey burst from the grass in a whirring roar—a dark blur of birds tearing the still cool air into noisy maelstrom with their stocky swift wings.

"Down!" Lee cried. "Down, Sad!"

Mr. Langston's double-barrel spoke, and a brown bird crumpled in mid-air.

Lee's gun was at his shoulder, and he was looking along the dark barrel, trying to pick a bird out of the crisscrossing, countless swift mass of them. Thousands of birds, it seemed! They would soon be too far. Faintly, he heard Sad barking, knew that he was racing after the quail. Desperately, Lee pressed the trigger.

But there was no shot, for he had forgotten to throw the

safety. He fumbled desperately for the little round, red-tipped device—and then it was too late.

Mr. Langston was watching the birds down. They were flying low now, fanning out, sailing level toward a pine thicket three hundred yards away.

"That was a pretty point," he said finally, "but he's got to be taught not to jump in like that. May have to put a leash on him when he starts trailing or winding." Then, having watched the covey settling in the pines off there, he turned to Lee. "You didn't shoot."

Lee shrugged lightly. "I plumb forgot the safety," he said, ashamed. "Must've been about a thousand birds came up!"

"It was a good covey, all right. Maybe twenty birds." Then the man laughed. "You're still pale, boy! Did you get a bird picked out to shoot at?"

"Never did. I guess I had wing fever, like deer hunters sometimes have buck fever."

"You'll get over that. Call Sad in to find the bird I shot."

The pup came racing back, much pleased with himself. Lee hugged him as before, bragged on him, patted his broad head.

"Don't make him *too* happy," Mr. Langston warned. "He may think one reason you're so pleased is that he jumped in and flushed the birds."

They moved over to the area where the bird had fallen. "Tell Sad 'Dead bird,'" Mr. Langston ordered. "Say it over and over and make him hunt close. He'll catch onto what you mean, finally."

Sad leaped about, yipping and wheeling, very proud of himself and eager for further commendation.

"Dead bird!" Lee kept saying, pointing into the grass and moving slowly about. "Dead bird! *Dead!*"

Sad yelped and ran circles as if trying hard to get into the spirit of the strange, new game.

"I see the bird," Mr. Langston said. "It's just this side of the persimmon sprout, there."

Lee looked hard, and at last saw the limp quail take shape against the perfectly blended background. He leaned over it, called, "Here, Sad! *Dead bird!*"

Getting Sad settled down to close hunting required at least five minutes. Lee brought the matter to a head by catching the setter's collar and pulling him to within a foot of the bird. "*Dead!*" he said softly. "Fetch!"

Sad caught the scent and dropped on a brief point. Then he lunged, barking hysterically at the bird. But he made no effort to touch it. He ran a swift circle about the still, brown form, darting in and then out, the while panting in excitement over the wondrous thing that had happened. Apparently, it was all too much for him.

"Pick up the bird," Mr. Langston said to Lee. "Pitch it out, as in the game you play with Sad. You've got to make him know that finding and bringing dead birds to you is one of his biggest jobs."

When Lee had tossed the bird a few feet away, Sad went for it, bounding happily, ears flopping. Then he proceeded to run some more circles about it. His barking was so frenzied that now and then he had to pause long enough to shake his head as if to relieve pain, or perhaps itching, set up in his ears by his own powerful voice.

"Here!" Lee ordered, holding out his hand. "Bring it here!"

Sad appeared to understand. He dived in and caught up the dead bird; then, of all things, he tossed it high and watched it fall into a clump of sedge. He leaped in and picked up the quail again, flung it farther than the first time.

"He looks pretty silly," Mr. Langston commented dryly, "but it takes time to train a bird dog. One of these days he'll find out what he's s'posed to do, and he'll be good at it. Why, one day he'll be bringing a dead bird to you, and he'll fall on point, likely on a single, with that dead bird in his mouth."

"How could he smell another bird with his mouth full of that very scent?" Lee marveled.

"I've always wondered. My Gordon did it twice. It's just more proof that there's a miracle built into a bird-dog's nose."

When Lee persisted in his efforts to make Sad bring him the dead bird, the setter pounced at it, then sprawled belly down, caught the quail between his big forefeet and started nipping at it, pulling out feathers.

"Now he sets out to *clean* the bird!" Mr. Langston exclaimed. "He gives complete service, doesn't he?"

They worked with Sad for a few minutes longer, but accomplished little. Each time he was persuaded to take the quail in his mouth, he either tossed it about or lay down and began pulling out feathers. So they gave it up for the time being and went after the singles in the pines.

Sad was hunting again, but he had some things to learn about scattered quail. This was different from following the massive scent of a covey, and he ran up two singles before the hunters were near enough to get shots.

"The main part of the covey is deeper in the pines," Mr. Langston said. "One or two usually drop early, like the ones he flushed."

Watching Sad, Lee realized how much experience meant in this branch of bird hunting. The dog must be ready to point at any moment, sometimes in mid-leap, coming down in a freeze, the body twisted grotesquely, according to the source of the suddenly caught scent. This was an intricate, demanding phase of the job that Sad must learn.

Another quail whirred up from a tangle of blackberry vines and swung to the left in erratic flight, dodging branches. There was no time for a shot.

"Hold it!" Lee begged as Sad fell on point, body twisted until he was almost looking at the tip of his rigid tail. "*Hold there!*"

"You take this shot," Mr. Langston offered. "If you miss, I'll try a long one."

This time, Sad waited until they were nearly up to him before he broke and lunged ahead. The bird came up fast and swung right. Lee's gun was at his shoulder, and his finger pressed the safety. Holding his breath, he swung to line up the ivory sight on the bird—then realized that he would be shooting too close to his father's head.

"Take 'im!" he gasped.

Mr. Langston shot quickly and missed. "You showed good sense," he said quietly. "If you'd shot, you'd have deafened me for a while."

They found no more of those singles.

Every once in a while, since leaving Mr. Branch, they had heard him shooting. Two and three quick shots marked a covey rise; then well-spaced single shots told of singles.

"If he's any good with a gun," Mr. Langston said, "he should have about two limits by this time."

"Boy, I'd like to bring in eight birds just one time!" Lee exclaimed.

"You will. It takes time for a beginning hunter as well as a beginning dog to get good. I'd hunted for two or three years before I could average eight or ten birds a day, and that was when there were a lot more birds than now."

They stopped for lunch under a big pine near the edge of a running branch. "We might as well take it easy for a while," Mr. Langston said. "Birds don't move much in the middle of the day. Sad needs to rest, anyway; he's not a hardened hunting dog yet."

Egg sandwiches and sausage and biscuits, some with generous helpings of homemade blackberry jam, tasted good to Lee. The pup had splashed noisily about in the stream, lapping the cold water eagerly, before coming near the big pine and settling on his haunches to watch the hunters eat. He sat there panting, red tongue dripping in eager hunger. Lee felt greedy and selfish. Then he tried to ease his conscience by tossing Sad a few morsels and watching him gulp them down, then whine and wag his tail for more.

"Don't feel bad," Mr. Langston advised. "If you fed him all he could eat right now, he wouldn't be fit to hunt this afternoon. A dog has to be treated like what he is."

"Yes, sir." Lee's agreement was not enthusiastic, and he deliberately looked away from the pleading pup as he finished his meal.

Aside from the feeling of shame Lee experienced in connection with his denial of Sad, there was nothing to mar that noontime. A cool breeze rustled the pine needles above them; now and then he heard the murmur of the shallow creek; a distant crow cawed raucously. But for these sounds the world was quiet. He and his father and his dog were away from the world, and there was the bright afternoon to anticipate.

Off there to the south, on and on, stretched the yellow sedge, its feathery tips trembling in the slow breeze. The vista extended on and on until the sedge-wrapped hills merged at last with the horizon. Here and there, a dark pine or an oak with frost-burnished leaves stood like a lonely sentinel keeping an endless watch. The sky was deep blue, tinged with faint lavender at the edge.

The boy let his imagination wander while his father dozed against the bole of the big pine. This was another world. This was free from work in hot fields, from school, from routine. This was a world exempt from man-made demands. Beneath the sedge, in the million labyrinths between the thick-grown bases of the clumps, were countless forms of life, each with its own ways and wants: tiny beetles and spiders and bugs, field mice, rabbits, grassbirds, quail, snakes and lizards now dormant in their lairs.

A sailing hawk almost as large as a buzzard interrupted his reverie. When it banked, to swing lower along the winding creek, the sun caught quick glints of white on the undersides of its wings. The graceful predator soon passed from Lee's sight, downstream, seeking some unwary prey.

Sad snuffled and made odd, throaty sounds. Lee looked that way and saw that the pup was asleep, dreaming. Lying on his side, he was twitching and fairly in a work. The foreleg and hindleg on the upper side were in motion, perfectly synchronized, as if running. The throaty sounds were growing into miniature barks. Clearly, Sad was dreaming of a chase.

"He's tired," Lee said softly, seeing his father stir.

The man yawned. "Good for him. Days like this will turn a pup into a dog. He needs hardening up."

"When is a bird dog at his best?" Lee asked. "How old, I mean."

"When he's three or four or five. It varies, like with people. Some dogs are at their best when they're getting along toward old. Eight or nine, say."

When the dreamed hunt was ended, Sad stood up and looked about, as if to get the world straightened out again. Then he turned around three times and flopped down, snuffled softly and went back to sleep.

Having rested for what seemed a very long time to Lee, they set out again. They swung left, starting a wide circle that would bring them back to the pickup at late afternoon.

It was almost an hour before Sad gave evidence of excitement. For one thing, he was covering less territory than in the morning; for another, weariness had dulled the edge of his eagerness. Now, instead of bounding and lunging this way and that, he had slowed to a trot. A half day would have been long enough to hunt him, Mr. Langston said, for he was just a pup. His first excited trailing of the afternoon ended when three field larks fluttered up and flew away. Sad did not run after them this time.

Somewhere around midafternoon, when they were halfway back to the truck, Sad struck a hot trail. After about ten minutes of crawling and creeping, he came down on a tight point at the edge of a persimmon thicket. This time—unaccountably, unless he was learning—he held the point until the hunters had passed him and flushed the covey. When they hurtled up from their covert, he leaped happily after them.

Lee was careful to flick off the safety this time, but he shot too soon. Under the stress of the roaring rise, he did not know when, or at exactly what bird, he shot. Something happened deep inside him every time quail wings sounded, and he wondered how anyone could pick out a bird calmly and shoot just at that one.

The old double spoke twice, and Lee saw two birds, yards apart, fold up and plummet downward.

"How'd you do it?" Lee cried. "I can't—"

"Shooting birds is like swimming or milking a cow," his father told him. "Once you've done it, you never forget. 'Course, I'm a little rusty now, out of practice, but there was a time when I was sharp enough to pick out two birds crossing and drop both with one shot."

"Well, we'll have one apiece for supper tonight," Lee said, pleased. "I hope Mama enjoys hers."

Again they worked with Sad, but he would not retrieve. He found both of the downed birds, pointed each one for a few seconds; but he refused to take a bird in his mouth. When Lee forced the second quail between the setter's teeth, Sad merely lay down and repeated the silly maneuver of plucking its feathers.

It was growing late when they reached the pickup. Having tied Sad in the bed, they drove homeward.

"We had a pretty good day," Lee said.

"Nice day," his dad agreed. "I've looked forward to it for a long time."

They said no more about it, for that was enough. Each knew how the other felt. Lee was keenly aware of the fact that he had not downed a bird; in fact, he had fired his new gun only once. Well, there was one good thing about that: the less he shot it, the longer his gun would last.

At home, Lee fed Sad and filled the water pan. Mr. Langston was showing him how to dress a quail when a strange car pulled up and stopped in the driveway. A tall, bareheaded young fellow slid out and went toward the front door.

"Around here, at the side of the house," Mr. Langston called. "Say, I believe that's Embry Wales."

The caller turned left and came toward them. He was slim,

with dark eyes and wavy, black hair. He moved easily, like a dancer or an athlete. "I am Embry," he said. "I see you got some birds. Have a good hunt?"

"We had a lot of hunt, all right," Mr. Langston told him, "but we brought in just three birds. Can't shake hands with you right now, but I'm glad to see you. How're things?"

"Could be worse, I reckon," Embry admitted. "Say, Lee, you're really growin', boy. How many did you knock down today?"

"Couldn't count 'em," Lee told him. "You have to have one to start countin', you know. But some day I'll—"

"Sure, you'll catch on. Takes practice." And, to Mr. Langston, "Thought I'd drive by and tell you that Mary Lou's out at her grandpa's now, and that he's better. She writes me a note every day."

"Well, that's nice. She's a fine girl, Mary Lou."

"You can say that again!" Embry agreed with feeling. "Never was one like her." Then he grinned self-consciously. "One of these days we're goin' to make old man Tomlin a great-grandpa. That ought to help things along."

"It would do more good than anything else on earth," Mr. Langston told him. "That old fellow's had a lot of grief and disappointment."

"I know that." Embry shrugged. "I can't rightly blame him for feelin' the way he does about me. Mary Lou was all he had left in the world that was worthwhile, and I took her away from him. To make it worse, I was a Wales. You know all about that side of it, though."

"Well, I know your dad and Mr. Tomlin, both being dog trainers, never did get along."

Embry laughed shortly. "My daddy had just one ambition,

and it never did come true: He wanted to beat Mr. Tomlin at the Great Southern Trials. Each year, he thought he had a dog that could turn the trick, but always there was a Tomlin setter that came out ahead of his dog. It got to be a mighty sore subject."

"The Tomlins were hard to beat," Mr. Langston declared. "I guess you picked up some things about dog training as you grew up."

"Yes, I worked with dogs 'til my daddy died. Went to field trials, and all that." And, bitterly, "Miles and miles we rode to the trials, full of hope; then, the same long miles, we went back home after the trials, sayin' nothin', my daddy and me, licked by some Tomlin setter." He paused, added, "But that's all over and done with. Say, I ran up on Guy Tomlin in town a while ago. He blustered around pretty big, threatened to whip me if I didn't go out and get Mary Lou and take her home with me."

"He scared you, I reckon," Mr. Langston offered.

"Well, I didn't climb a tree. Fact, I invited him to come on and start the whippin' job, but he just big-talked some more. You know why I think he wants Mary Lou away from out there?"

"Not exactly. You s'pose he wants to do the old man harm?"

"Oh, I don't figure he wants to do him bodily harm," Embry said slowly, "but from the hints he dropped, I think he wants to have the old fellow judged crazy and sent off to the asylum. Then Guy could take over the place. He'd sell it, the first chance he got."

"That's about as bad as bodily harm," Mr. Langston declared. "But the fact is, he'll have a tough time proving it except that he's a little 'touched' himself." Then, carelessly, "Did Guy mention the setter pup that old man Tomlin gave Lee?"

"He did. In fact, he says he'll get that pup if it's the last thing he does."

"Now, I hope it doesn't come to that," Mr. Langston said slowly. "Guy's too young a man to be figuring on doing his last deed!"

Embry laughed. "He's just a lot of big talk. Lee, how 'bout showin' me your pup? I've never seen him."

Out at the pen, while Sad was noisy and active over the attention, Lee told Embry about the hunt. "Sad made a couple of good points, and on his first day out!" he finished proudly.

"That's mighty good," Embry said. "Boy, I like to hunt birds, but it's been so, the last few years, that I couldn't do much of it. Could I go with you some time? I get Saturdays off."

"How about next Saturday?" Lee invited him. "Maybe you can show me how to smooth down some of Sad's rough edges."

Another car was pulling up near the front gate. When the driver crawled out, Lee could see, in spite of the poor light, that it was Guy Tomlin.

"Come on," Embry said quickly, for he had also recognized the caller. "Let's join your dad and make up a good welcoming committee!"

Guy Tomlin came almost to the front gate before calling out, "Hello! Hurd Langston?"

"Come around here, Guy," Mr. Langston called. "Around here, at the side of the house."

"Maybe you better come out here," the man called. "You can read this paper in my car lights."

The three of them, Mr. Langston ahead, went toward the front-yard gate. Guy Tomlin was standing in front of his car, a sheet of white paper in his hand.

"What's written there?" Mr. Langston inquired as he led the way through the gate and onto the right-of-way.

"You can read it," Guy Tomlin said. "It's pretty plainly wrote out. I've come to git that setter pup, an' I ain't foolin' around this time. Fact is, I'm in sort of a hurry."

Lee's heart was flying. Hot and cold waves chased each other up and down his back. He bit his lip, holding hot words that begged to be said.

Guy Tomlin, holding the paper so that it was clearly visible in the lights of his car, waited for them to come up. "This instrument," he stated in the tone of a person confident of advantage, "tells you to turn that dog over to me. It's signed by my father."

"I've got a paper, too," Lee put in quickly. "It says that Black Saddle belongs to me. Mr. Tomlin wrote and signed it."

"I figured you'd have somethin'," the man said sharply, "but my paper's newer." He peered beyond Mr. Langston at the slim figure of Embry Wales, apparently not recognizing him. "I didn't come here to git mobbed," he declared in a high voice. "I come in a friendly way, to settle this legal an' to git what's mine by rights." He shook the paper until it rattled, holding it toward Mr. Langston. "See here?"

"I see what you're holding," Mr. Langston told him, speaking quietly. "And we're not bad about mobbing people. Why're you so set on beating Lee out of that pup, Guy?"

"Because he's my dog, that's why. Besides, I'm gettin' back

in the trainin' business. Already, I'm handlin' a fine string of pointers for Dr. Eddley, in Memphis. But I want a dog of my own, 'specially that last Tomlin dog." He folded the paper, stuck it into his shirt pocket. "We're a-wastin' time, Hurd. I'm in pretty much of a hurry to get back to Memphis, so—"

"We're not in much of a hurry," Mr. Langston interrupted, still speaking gently, almost sympathetically. "To be right honest, Guy, I believe your paper is a forgery."

"Oh, you *do?*" The man yelped the words with an air of righteous anger. "Well, let me tell you somethin', Hurd Langston, when a man accuses me of . . ."

"I saw the handwritin'," Lee broke in, "and it's not the same as the one on my paper, which old Mr. Tomlin wrote out."

"You stay outa this, boy. I'm dealin' with your daddy. You're a minor, anyway."

Embry came into the light then. His slim face was pale, and his mouth was set hard. "You've pestered these folks long enough, Guy," he said. "Now, get in your car, and I'll follow you to the Tomlin place. If Mr. Luke says that Sad's your dog, we'll come back here, and I'll tell Mr. Langston and Lee. They'll take my word for it."

"Shut up an' mind your own business!" Guy Tomlin snapped. "Pa won't do business with you, nohow."

"Forget about that. I'll follow you over there, and we'll get this thing settled once and for all."

"I don't have no time for that. I'm in a hurry to get back to Memphis, an' I want that dog now." He was backing toward the door of his car as Embry advanced slowly toward him. "Don't you start no trouble," he warned. "You push me too far, Embry Wales, an' I'll mop up this here road right-of-way with you."

"I've heard the wind blow before," Embry said, taking a quick step forward. "Now, you get *goin'*!"

"Who're you to order me around?" Guy Tomlin asked, backing into the open door of his car. "Why, I'll—"

"You'd better go, Guy," Mr. Langston said helpfully. "Seems Embry means business. And you listen to this: you come back here for the same purpose again, I'll swear out a warrant against you for disturbing the peace."

"Why, I ain't lifted my hand," the man said in a grieved tone. "It's a downright lie! I ain't—"

"And if you try to put old man Tomlin away somewhere," Mr. Langston added, "you'll wind up in a peck of trouble. I can find a hundred men who'll swear that the old man has more sense than you've got!"

"Now, *git!*" Embry ordered sharply. "Take off, or I'll make you start moppin' up this right-of-way with me."

Guy Tomlin *got*. In fact, he fell under the wheel and fairly scratched off.

"He'd better watch it," Lee said, looking appreciatively at Embry, "or he'll be picked up again for speeding!"

✼ 7 ✼

UNDER THE LEADERSHIP OF MR. LANGSTON AND MR. WEBB, THE Riptonville Hunting and Fishing Club was organized the next week. There were, Mr. Langston reported the next morning, about fifty men at the courthouse in response to the "Calling All Sportsmen" ad in the county weekly.

"Did you elect officers?" Lee asked. "Hope they made you president, as hard as you've worked on this thing."

"No, we got Mr. Hayward to be temporary chairman, and he appointed a committee to write up a constitution and by-laws. Elections will come later, and I don't want any office. I'll do better, easing around in the background, quiet-like. By the way, Mr. Andrews and Joe Ray came to the meeting. Joe was pretty busy shaking hands for votes next summer." He nodded, pleased. "It's working out just right."

On the following Wednesday, when Lee came in from school, he learned that his mother and father had been over to the Tomlin place.

"It's spick as well as span," his mother told him. "Mary Lou's really doing a wonderful job out there. The setup is fine for Mr. Tomlin, who looks better than in years; but it's right hard on Mary Lou and Embry to have to live this way."

"Did you tell him about the forged paper?" Lee asked his father.

"No. He'd have just felt bad about something he couldn't help. Anyway, Guy seems to have given up on it, since we haven't heard from him in several days. When I mentioned that Guy spoke of getting into dog training, the old fellow didn't seem to be impressed."

"Say, why can't we have him over here for Christmas dinner?" Lee asked eagerly. "I could show him how Sad hunts—taking him in the pickup, I mean, for a short round. And it would give Mary Lou and Embry a chance to be together."

"Why, that's a fine idea!" Mrs. Langston agreed with a proud look at Lee. "You know, I honestly believe the old man would give in if Embry would do something to prove himself —something Mr. Tomlin would admire."

"What could that be?" asked Lee.

"I haven't the faintest idea." Then she laughed briefly. "The only thing I can think of that he'd admire would be the winning of first place in some important field trial. That kind of language Mr. Luke Tomlin understands."

Early on Saturday Embry came, eager for a bird hunt. Mr. Langston had business in town, so Lee and Embry drove to the territory that Lee and his father had hunted on the previous Saturday.

Released, Sad coursed out wide, heading for the place where he had found the first covey a week before.

"He knows right where he is," Lee said proudly. "That's pretty smart!"

"He moves with class," Embry declared. "Sad'll be a real dog, Lee."

In less than ten minutes Sad was trailing. They hurried after him.

"Easy, boy!" Lee kept calling. "Easy, now!"

Sad was too eager. It had been a long week for him, too, with the excitement of anticipation building up in him. Crawling, he topped the rise, then fell on point. But he held for only a few seconds before lunging ahead, barking wildly.

The covey wheeled up and fanned out toward the pine thicket that had been their refuge the other time.

"You do the yellin'," Embry suggested. "Just one fellow should give a huntin' dog his orders, 'specially a learnin' dog."

"He's too anxious, after being penned up for a week," Lee explained.

"Sure, he is. An' that's all right." Embry shouldered his 12-gauge pump. "The pretty part of it is that he *wants* to hunt, an' he knows what he's huntin'. Just got to learn some manners, that's all."

In the pines Sad ran up a single, then, two lunges beyond that misfortune, dropped on a tight point.

"Pretty!" Embry whispered. "Never saw a classier point. You take this one. Put the bead right on him, an' take your time. Shoot a little ahead of him if he swings to the side."

As usual, Lee was excited over the point, and he was breathless over the unpredictability of a quail that might burst up from any nearby cover and change from a hidden, silent thing into a hurtling blur of brown feathers and noise. Gun ready, he walked in.

The bird whipped up from almost between the boy's feet and veered to the right. Its line of flight was upward, toward dark branches that would offer protection.

The swift bird was a blur as Lee brought his gunstock against his shoulder. He saw a flash of white on the small head, knew that it was a rooster, and wondered how he could

The bird veered to the right

be aware of so small a detail when the whole bird was so hard
to put his ivory bead on.

Now! He pressed the trigger, and even as he touched the
curved metal he sensed that he had chosen the exact split-
second. There had been no time for thinking—only for *feeling,* a strange flash of *knowing* . . .

The lone bird crumpled and plunged into the carpet of
pine needles and grass.

"Good shot!" Embry cried. "That was knockin' 'im!"

Lee was shaking throughout. So easy! He stood there, as
still as Sad had been on point, eyes glued to the spot where
the bird had fallen.

"Something told me to press the trigger," he said slowly,
not exactly talking to Embry. "It was so easy!"

"It always seems easy," Embry said, "when the bird falls."
The words seemed to Lee to reach him from a great distance
as he stood there, eyes still holding the spot where the brown
bird had fallen. A sense of remorse, which he had not expected, had come over him. It was his first deliberate taking
of a life. He looked at Embry, who was standing still, watching him, and he wondered if Embry knew just how he felt.

"I just shot out there," Lee said slowly, "sort of toward
the bird, and he went down."

"It was a good, clean shot," Embry said. "It seemed easy,
but when you miss a half dozen straight some day you'll
wonder what was easy about it." Then Embry smiled, nodded,
said, "I know just how you feel, Lee. Don't try to tell me.
Every kid with his first gun feels just like you—proud, sorry,
thrilled, ashamed. Come on, le's make Sad retrieve this one."

Embry worked patiently at this assignment, and gently.
Finally, after Sad had gone through his earlier maneuvers of

tossing the limp bird about and of picking its feathers while holding it tightly between his forepaws, Embry forced the bird into his mouth, held it closed lightly over the body and led the setter to Lee.

"Take it from him," Embry ordered. "Then pet him and brag on him. He'll catch on."

Lee took the quail from Sad and then did as Embry had suggested. The pup whined and leaped about, pleased to have such recognition.

"At least, he won't be a bird-crusher," Embry predicted. "Lots of dogs fairly chew up a bird, bringin' it in."

Sad pointed two more singles, both of which fell to Embry's gun. Each time, as before, Embry forced him to retrieve after finding the bird.

"He'll be a dandy!" Embry said, pleased, when Sad had carried the second bird to Lee, without having his jaws held together on their feathered burden. "This pup ought to be a field-trial winner some of these days. With the right trainin', I mean."

"Which field trial?" Lee asked.

"Maybe even the Great Southern." Embry shook his head slowly. "You know, my dad never did take a top place there. Mr. Tomlin always licked him."

They had a good hunt that day. Embry downed six of the eight birds they brought in. Lee's second bird had fallen on a covey rise, and the boy had to admit that he had just shot wildly.

"I can't pick out one on the rise," he said, disgusted. "I just can't. When they fly up, with all that roarin' and flutterin' of wings, I paralyze! I just shot toward the dark commotion in the air, and one fell."

"Bird huntin's a funny business," Embry said. "It takes a long time for the hunter to settle down and do a good job; so we ought to be patient about a dog. Think how much he has to learn!"

Mr. Tomlin had Christmas dinner with the Langstons. They drove over and brought him to their house; and, while Mrs. Langston was finishing last-minute preparations, Lee and his father took the old fellow down along the foot of the sedge ridge.

When Mr. Tomlin saw Sad lope up the rise, moving effortlessly through the waist-high, tan sedge, tail thrashing tirelessly, he said, "That's the picture I'll take to my grave! It could be fifty years ago—but 'course this automobile don't belong in the picture."

"I wish he'd point," Lee said. "If you could see him come down on a covey—"

"I know just how he'd look," Mr. Tomlin broke in. "I've seen too many of his kind. His head, back an' tail make a straight line, except that his tail curves up a little at the tip. That right?"

"It's exactly right," Lee told him. "That's just the way he looks when he points."

"With the right trainin'," the old man said, "he'll be a great dog. I can tell. An' don't let 'im be wasted, Lee. Hunt 'im a lot. An' always work with him patient-like. Why, he's got the stuff to win the Great Southern one of these days."

"What would that be worth to me?" Lee inquired, trying to sound businesslike.

"Well, your dog's picture would be in the paper, an' so would yours, maybe. On top of that, you'd have a pile of cash money in your pocket. An' more than that, you'd have a lot of offers from moneyed fellows who'd want to buy your dog."

"That's silly!" Lee said with undue feeling. "Sad's not for sale for any price."

"I know that, son, but they don't know it. There are plenty of rich fellows in the cities who'll spend thousands of dollars just to have a winnin' dog to their names. To tell the truth, they don't even hunt birds. They just want to be known as sportsmen, a lot of 'em, I mean."

Sad made no point for Mr. Tomlin, but his style was a refreshing sight to the old man. "It puts me back to years an' years ago," he said softly as they drove back to the house.

Late that afternoon they took Mr. Tomlin home. Nothing had been said during the day about either Guy Tomlin or Embry Wales. When they came in sight of the Tomlin house, they could see a bright light from the fireplace. Mary Lou had returned from spending Christmas Day with Embry.

"It was awful nice," the old man told Mrs. Langston. "I thank you, ma'am, an' I'm sure Mary Lou does, too."

"We liked having you," Mrs. Langston said. "And I know that Mary Lou enjoyed being with Embry today."

This time, Mr. Tomlin said nothing for or against Embry Wales. He ignored the reference completely, not even permitting himself the luxury of a disgusted snort.

As they drove back home, Mrs. Langston said, "I think he's weakening a little. Some day it'll get straightened out. You watch."

The Hunting and Fishing Club was well under way by January. Mr. Hayward had been elected president, with Hurd Langston as vice president. Mr. Joe Ray—in a clever move by "string-pullers"—had been chosen treasurer.

A project to increase interest in the club was announced in late January. There would be a puppy field trials just before the end of the bird season. The local paper gave it full publicity, and the Memphis papers picked it up. The angle was that sportsmen of the Tiptonville area, long famous for its bird-hunting advantages, were seeking to bring back some of the interest of the old days.

"Who spark-plugged this?" Lee asked his father on the evening of the day the announcement appeared.

"Mr. Hayward and I thought it might be a good idea. It sort of grew from there."

"How about letting Embry handle Sad in the meet?" Lee asked. "If he wins, it may help straighten things out between him and Mr. Tomlin."

"That's up to you to decide," Mr. Langston told him. "You may have something there."

Mrs. Langston was sure that Lee had something there. "That poor old man," she said, "is just waiting for an excuse to make up with Embry. He needs a son about as much as any man could, and part of his hardheadedness comes from the simple fact that he's so very lonesome."

Embry was pleased when Lee asked him to handle Sad in the forthcoming puppy trials. "We'll show that crowd," he declared, "what a real pup can do! They'll take their potlickers and sneak home."

For the next week or more, Embry was out late every afternoon to work with Sad. "I won't touch him with a switch or a stick," he promised Lee, "but I'll bellow mighty loud at the hardheaded rascal."

"I'm not worried about how you handle him. How do you s'pose he'll act with other dogs around?"

"That's the very thing that bothers me," Embry confessed. "He's never hunted with another dog, an' they'll be sent out in pairs at the trials. Besides that part of it, there'll be dozens of dogs there, whinin' an' barkin' an' just being dogs. No tellin' how ol' Sad'll come through that kind of excitement."

"Well, if he doesn't win, he'll learn some things," Lee said, privately sure that Sad would win top prize. "It'll be good for him, anyway."

At last, the day of the puppy trials came, and with it came bird hunters and their dogs from all directions. Trainers were on hand with their prize charges; breeders and dealers were there to sell and buy; hunters without dogs were on hand just to watch the competition.

Early that morning Mary Lou brought Mr. Tomlin to headquarters. Men who knew him by past connection or by reputation gathered about him for advice or just for talk. Tall and lean, wearing a rusty black suit that withering time had made too large for him, and topped by a wide-brimmed black felt hat, old Luke Tomlin moved happily among men and dogs. He was reliving in some measure the great days that were gone.

Mr. Flem Branch was there with the young liver-and-white pointer that Lee had seen on the day of Sad's fight with the big "rip-rap." And Guy Tomlin was out from Memphis with two young pointers from Dr. Eddley's kennels. Riptonville reeked of dogs and teemed with men who lived and breathed dogs.

Sad was trembling with the excitement of it all. Lee was sure that he tried to bark reply to every yip and whine from crates and trucks.

Despite the fact that Guy would be in the competition,

Mr. Tomlin agreed to serve as one of the judges. Mr. Hayward would serve with him.

Sad was released for his first heat, teamed with an Irish setter named Big Mack, a handsome, rangy fellow with a rich, deep-chestnut coat. The Llewellyn lost no time in proving that the misgivings Lee and Embry had held were well-grounded. He was far more interested in the Irish setter than he was in hunting birds. The red one swung to the right, heading for a birdy draw, and Sad was right beside him. He was barking and leaping about, racing out in front of the Irish setter, crouching and begging. It was clear that he had no intention of wasting this golden chance for a romp.

Lee groaned. "The big simpleton!" he wailed to his father and Embry, who were standing together at the front of the crowd. "Just look at him!"

Mr. Langston said nothing—with words, that is. His expression of disgust said much. Embry was standing slumped against the bed of a pickup truck. As he watched the pair, he chewed on a match stem, the muscles at the point of his lean jaw bunching hard and often.

Big Mack wheeled on Sad once, growling a threat, but the black-and-white ignored the rebuff by running a few gay circles and barking in his biggest voice. He was determined to tease his businesslike friend into a frolicking romp.

Then, worst of all, when the big red one winded birds and began coursing them, Sad streaked in ahead and flushed the covey. And, by way of capping it off, he chased them, bellowing as if in a hysteria of pride over his dramatic handling of the matter.

The laughter and the comments of the men added to Lee's mounting misery. His face was white, so that the scattering of fine freckles across his nose stood out in sharp relief. He was not sure whether he felt better or worse when he heard Mr. Tomlin chuckle and say, "Now, there's a slap-happy Tomlin dog for you!"

Sad did not make a find that day. He continued at every chance to work hard at forming friendships with other dogs, with frantic barkings as he leaped and frisked about. A stranger remarked dryly in Lee's hearing, "Well, this is a puppy trials, ain't it?"

At late afternoon Lee and Mr. Langston took Sad home and fastened him in the pen. Neither had anything to say about what had happened. This was Lee's worst disappointment in Black Saddle, the last Tomlin.

"Far's I'm concerned," he told his mother, "I don't care. I'm just sorry—"

"You do care, too," she broke in. "I care and your daddy cares. The only one who doesn't care is Sad. Now, what were you about to say?"

"That I'm sorry for Embry's sake. He's spent so much time on our box-headed, good-time Charlie!"

There was another reason for regret the next day. A slim pointer, handled by Guy Tomlin, had taken first place in the trials.

"That proves one thing," Mr. Langston said dryly. "Old man Tomlin was a mighty fair judge!"

The bird season ended. Nine months of no hunting lay ahead. Lee had hoped he would feel safe in letting Sad run free at least a part of the long period of three seasons that must pass before it was time to hunt again. After what had happened at the puppy trials, though, he was afraid. Sad would likely go traipsing off somewhere, seeking friends. Or he might spend his boundless energy in chasing cars along the highway. Another thing, if Sad were free to roam, there would always be the danger that he would be picked up and carried away.

Black Saddle was a handsome dog now, tall and long-feathered behind forelegs and along the underside of his tail. He had yet to deepen at chest, to thicken at shoulder and haunch; but any man who knew setters could see in Sad the beautiful dog he would be. The safe thing would be to keep him in his pen.

Ducks and geese went north, sprawling along the sky, their tireless wings fanning out the message that winter was ending. Spring was showing through. Small thunderheads formed along the horizon, then disappeared without building into storms. Pear trees burst into bloom, snow-white against the pale green of young leaves. Plum thickets were soft banks of snowy blossom along fence rows and ditch banks. In the pastures, tiny, four-petaled lavender stars bloomed deep within the grass. Redbuds flamed into spires and fronds of purplish-red as if to warm the woods for the more cautious blossomers. Along yard fences jonquils broke out their bells of rich yellow that swayed and nodded in the breeze. Hyacinths pushed their rich spikes, quickly bursting into bloom, out of the warming clay. Spring had surely come, but there would be cold snaps yet.

Time ran into field work and warm days. April showers raced across the land, with sharp lightning and crackling thunder. Early corn was up in streaks of pale green to mark the drills. Birds were busy with nest-building. A quick "sassy" wren, Lee noted, was flying straw to an eave corner of the Langston house.

Maybe it was "blackberry winter" that came in late April, with a roaring blast out of the north. It struck at midafternoon, and the wind held until past sunset, an indication that it would likely continue to blow throughout the night. This would be good, for there would be no frost.

Some time deep in the night Lee awoke suddenly. He thought he had been aroused by Sad's barking, but there was now no sound from the pen. He went to his window and looked out into the black night. The wind was blowing in sharp gusts from the north. No cars were on the highway. Lee stood there for a few minutes, shivering in the cold, listening, hearing nothing. Then he went back to bed.

As he drowsed off, he thought he heard a car starting up in the distance, toward town. He went to sleep.

It was cold the next morning, but there had been no frost.

Lee went to the kitchen window and looked toward the dog pen, but Sad was not in sight. No wonder, though, as cold as it was, that he was staying in his little house. It was a shame that he had to be kept imprisoned like this week after week. If he could run and rip, he'd be in better shape when the season came again. Mustn't feed him too heavily this summer, now that he was grown, or he'd go into the fall fat and lazy. A hunting dog, Lee knew, should be lean.

After breakfast, Lee stirred up a pan of food for Sad and took it to the pen. At the gate, he called, "Sad! Here, fella!"

But nothing happened. Usually the setter came bounding out when summoned. In fact, he seldom had to be summoned, for he almost always heard the back door close and was at the gate, barking, when Lee arrived there. This had been true, even during bird season, when he was weary from hunting.

Lee set the pan down quickly and went in. He stooped and looked into the doghouse—knowing at the same time that such looking was not necessary—and found it empty.

Lee straightened up and began searching along the top strand of barbed wire for a tag of hair that would mark Sad's point of departure. He went along the fence slowly, examining each barb carefully. Halfway around the fence, and on the side nearest the road, he stopped abruptly. There it was! The wire had been cut. Each small section of the poultry wire had been neatly snipped by a thief who had come prepared for the job. A tag of black hair, likely from Sad's back, clung to a ragged end of wire.

Lee stood there, breathing hard. This was worse than when Sad had leaped the fence and joined the foxhounds! Now the setter was in possession of someone who had taken trouble and risk to get him, who would be determined to keep him.

The weeds on the outside of the fence had been trampled down, but there were no footprints in the deep Bermuda grass, of course.

Lee wheeled and started for the house. At first he ran. Then he stopped. There was no need now to run. "It happened when I heard him barkin' in the night," he told himself. "The car I heard start up was the one that took him away."

Lee went on toward the back door. He would be calm when he took the bad news into the house. He would be grown-up about it. He would go in and say simply, "Well it's happened. Sad was stolen last night."

❦ 8 ❧

When lee came back into the kitchen, mrs. langston turned from the sink and saw his white face. "Mercy!" she exclaimed. "You're so pale. What's wrong?"

"Somebody stole Sad last night."

"What?" Mr. Langston called from the dining room. "How do you know he was stolen?"

"The fence is cut, and he's gone."

"I knew Guy Tomlin wouldn't quit 'til he got the dog!" Mrs. Langston declared. "He's a scound—"

"Easy, Nell," Mr. Langston interrupted, coming into the kitchen. "We don't know who did it. Come on, Lee."

"But we know how determined he was to have Sad," she said as they went out.

They hurried toward the enclosure. Lee led the way around to the place where the wire had been cut. In the heavy grass and weeds between the fence and the edge of the right-of-way, they could trace the course of the marauder. At the edge of the road there was hard-packed gravel, so tracks were not visible there.

"He went straight onto the concrete," Mr. Langston said. "He knew this packed gravel would show no tracks. Pretty sharp!"

They went along the highway, toward Riptonville, searching the shoulder carefully for tread marks, for the thief must have parked at the edge of the road while he carried out his plan.

A hundred yards down the highway, Lee spotted tire impressions in the damp clay of the shoulder. "Reckon he parked this far from the pen?" he asked.

"I'd guess that he did, but these might've been left by just anybody. It hasn't rained in a day or two; fact, longer than that."

They looked along the clay shoulders for another hundred yards, but found no more tread marks. Returning to the house, Mr. Langston called the sheriff.

"You'd better bring out a camera," he suggested, "plus the sharpest detective you've got. We want that dog back."

Within thirty minutes Sheriff Taylor, accompanied by the deputy in charge of photography and fingerprinting, had arrived at the Langston place. The tire marks Lee had found were carefully photographed, and irregularities in both front and rear tires on the right side were established.

"It's not the best evidence on earth," the sheriff pointed out, "but we'll work on it."

It was, of course, a thin hope. The tires that had left the marks could at that moment be whizzing along hundreds of miles from the Langston place, bearing Sad farther and farther from home. Or the thief could be in some town or city, Sad well concealed, the tires safely changed.

"Or the tire marks," Mr. Langston pointed out, "could've been made by a car whose owner had nothing to do with it. Boy, it *is* a thin chance we're working on."

The sheriff had made no mention of Guy Tomlin, but he

had said, "We've all got our own private suspicions, I guess, but we can't accuse anybody without mighty good proof. Having a character-damage suit popped on you wouldn't be any fun." Then he added, in what could have been taken as a vague promise, "We do have some connections here and there, you know."

Embry came out when he heard the bad news. He was sure that Guy Tomlin was at the bottom of the dirty business. "He did it, or he hired it done," Embry summed it up tersely.

"Let's keep the news from old Mr. Tomlin," Mrs. Langston said. "He'd feel mighty bad about it, even if he's not responsible for what Guy does."

Embry nodded. " 'Course, he'll be sorry it happened, but I don't think he takes much blame for Guy bein' a low-down skunk!" Then he brightened. "Mary Lou's back with me now. We just couldn't keep on livin' the way we did last winter."

"Certainly you couldn't," Mrs. Langston agreed. "She goes back out to see about the old fellow now and then, I guess."

"Every few days. An' he's just as ornery as ever—which shows he's in fine health."

Of course, it was not long before news of the theft reached Mr. Tomlin. As soon as possible after he had heard of it, Mary Lou brought him to see the Langstons. "You'll get your dog back," he told Lee confidently. "May take a long time, but the Tomlin dogs always come home."

"But stolen things can be carried farther away, and faster, than they used to be," Lee reminded him.

"That's for sure," the old man agreed. "But what I said still holds. The gran'daddy of Sad, four or five generations back —le's see, that was ol' Luke the First—was carried off once.

It was over a hundred miles, but soon's he got loose he made a break for home. He got there, too."

"Over a hundred miles?" Lee asked, taking heart.

"Yes, siree!" The Tomlin brows waggled, as they usually did when he bragged on Tomlin dogs. "Those big setters carry compasses in their heads. They'll go through fire an' water to get back to their masters. Ol' Luke, we found out later, had swum two rivers an' a lake on his way home."

This was comforting news to Lee, but as time passed without bringing any news of Sad, he began to lose confidence. The fact that Luke the First had made it home was no assurance that Sad the First might do the same thing.

April ran into May, then hot June came. Morning after morning, Lee had dressed hurriedly and gone out at daybreak, or a little later, to see if Sad had returned during the night.

"Go on and get your sleep," Mrs. Langston told him finally. "You know that as soon as Sad gets home, he'll wake us all up with his barking. Whether it's day or night, he'll do that."

"Yes'm." Lee let it go at that. There was no need to mention his dwindling hopes, based on the reasoning that good dogs are kept penned up during off-season time. Sad would have little chance to make a break for home; of that Lee was sure.

Then another bit of dismal reasoning: During all the time since the night of the theft, Sad may have come to like his new home. And between now and the next bird season, which would likely be his first chance to escape, Sad might even forget the place where he had grown up. Perhaps he was with other dogs now, and happy over it. There was also the grave possibility that he liked his new master.

"A fellow goes through a lot in raising a dog," Mr. Langston said one night as they sat on the front porch and rested from a hot day in the field. "Lots of times, it turns out like this, one way or another."

"Let's keep on remembering what Mr. Tomlin said," Mrs. Langston begged. "No matter how long it takes him to make the break for home, he'll do it when the time comes."

"I kind of think he's right about it," Mr. Langston said slowly. Then, after a long pause, for it was an awkward thing to have to say, yet it needed saying, "Another side of it we've got to look at is that Sad may not make it home at all. Might as well face that, while we're talking about it. You'll find another dog you'll like, Lee. It won't be like Sad, of course, for a fellow's first dog is always his best one, I guess. But we'll have us a bird dog of some kind, come next season."

"Yes, sir," Lee said. That was all he could risk saying right then, for the hot lump he had felt before was crowding into his throat. Time had helped a little; and, too, he was growing up, being now almost as tall as his father and growing wide at the shoulders. He swallowed, to make the lump go away. "Even if Sad gets loose and tries to get home, a thousand things can happen to him. He's wearin' a new collar now, with no tellin' whose name on it, and we'll never know how he wound up."

"What if he does come home, wearing a new collar?" Mrs. Langston put in. "I hadn't thought of that. It would tell us who the thief was, wouldn't it?"

"That's right, it would!" Lee agreed excitedly. "That'd be real justice, wouldn't it?"

When Mr. Winston returned to Riptonville to make final negotiations for hunting rights on enough acreage to justify the promotion he had planned, he discovered that things had been happening. A special meeting of the Hunting and Fishing Club was promptly called, and the promoter was invited to attend. Mr. Langston was in town until late that night.

"The whole thing was a shock to Mr. Winston," he reported at breakfast the next morning. "He came here, all primed up with a lot of borrowed money and a stock-selling scheme. Did he sputter and spew when he learned that there wasn't a landowner who'd sell hunting rights on his land!"

"I guess," Mrs. Langston said, "that you and Jim Webb feel pretty smart about this whole thing, don't you?"

"Yes, ma'am, we do. And so does every other man here who wants to keep this country the way it was intended to be. As it stands now, Lee and all the other boys around here can ramble these hills and hollows without being told by outsiders where they can or can't hunt." He grinned briefly. "It was a pretty sharp scheme, the way we worked everything his bedside radio, turned the volume low to keep from disout—if I do say so myself!"

During the hot, dry spell in late August, Lee was awake early one morning, just as day was breaking. He switched on turbing his mother and father. A farm newscast was on, coming out of Memphis. Dressing slowly, dreading the scorcher that was coming up, Lee paid little attention to what the man was saying about late-summer boll weevil control:

"And now, ladies and gentlemen of the Live-at-Home audience," the announcer said, winding up, "all of us like a dog story. This one comes to us from up at Lindenwood. A shaggy dog, described by some as black and white, by others as brindle, had been playing hobo at various back doors—"

Lee stopped dead-still, one leg of his levis on, his heart racing . . .

"He barks in a friendly manner," the announcer went on,

"begging for hand-outs; then he gulps down whatever is tossed to him and disappears at top speed. An interesting feature of the story is that the dog appears at only the houses that are well off the main highway, and only at places where there are boys."

The voice paused there, leaving Lee tense and straining to hear more.

"Just thought you'd like this mystery-dog tale, folks. If more news of the wary hobo comes in, I'll pass it on to you."

"It's Sad!" Lee gasped. Then he leaped into the rest of his clothes and went downstairs.

Mr. Langston was not visibly excited—perhaps a pretense to ease possible disappointment. "He didn't even say it was a setter, did he?" the man asked.

"Not exactly," Lee confessed. "But it's a shaggy dog, and it acts just the way Sad would act if he was makin' his way back home. Le's go to Lindenwood this very mornin'."

"It'd be like chasing a will-o'-the-wisp."

"But if it *is* Sad, we've got to find him. What if he gets hungry and starts killin' chickens? Then he'll get shot."

They drove to Lindenwood, a farm community a hundred miles north of Memphis. After making inquiries, they found a farmhouse where the hobo dog had scrounged a meal.

"He could've been black and white," the woman said. "He was so muddy. No, I don't know which-a-way he went from here . . . Yes, I think there was some black on his face. He sure ate like a starved thing!"

After driving over miles of winding country road southeast of Lindenwood, blowing the horn in the remote hope that Sad would hear and recognize it, they returned home. Lee was miserable.

For the following three mornings he was up at daybreak,

his radio turned on. The third morning, after important matters were out of the way, the announcer said:

"And now, neighbors, here's another chapter in our hobo-dog serial. An amusing account has just come in from Elm Corner, south of Lindenwood. From there we hear that the dog is marked like a Llewellyn. Shortly after dawn yesterday morning he appeared at the residence of Wesley Barnes. When Joey, the teen-age Barnes' son, went out to feed the gaunt tramp, a big bronze gobbler came strutting around the house, and the dog promptly took off in high gear. Apparently, he finds himself allergic to turkeys."

"It *is* Sad!" Lee cried. "Remember how Mrs. Wharton's gobbler worked him over that day? Now I know it's Sad!"

"A lot of pups have been whipped by gobblers," Mr. Langston reminded him. "One thing about it, though, that dog's making good time southward. Elm Corner is about forty miles this side of Lindenwood."

"What if the thief's hearin' these reports, too?" Lee asked, worried. "If Sad's wearin' a collar that'll tell who the thief is, then he'll try to catch or kill the dog!"

Mr. Langston agreed to the logic of this, but he refused to drive to Elm Corner. "There's no use," he said. "The way that tramp dog's traveling, he's miles from there by this time."

It was dreadful to sit around and do nothing, so Lee wrote a letter to Joey Barnes:

Dear Joey:

The radio announcer that talks about the tramp dog up your way has just finished his broadcast about how the dog ran from a turkey gobbler. I am sure that it is my dog, who was stolen from his pen back of our house during the cool snap in April. Will you write and answer these questions, and please be careful, for I want to know for sure it's my dog, so that if it is not I can stop worrying and hoping that it is.

Was the tramp dog tall and big-boned and black and white?

Was there a big patch of black along his back? Like a saddle, I mean.

Was one side of his face black and the other side white? My dog was, or is, marked that way. It makes him look like a clown.

When he was begging for something to eat, did he thrash his tail from side to side, and did he crouch and bark? And after barking did he shake his head, flopping his big ears, as if to ease the pain or the itching in them caused by the barking? My dog does that.

Was the underside of the tramp dog's tail sort of like a plume? With long, fine white hair, I mean. And the same back of his forelegs?

Was the dog's coat curly, 'specially along the neck and back?

Could you tell if the dog's eyes were kind and friendly? My dog's eyes are like that.

And when he ran from the gobbler, did he look back over his shoulder, with his ears laid back and the whites of his eyes showing?

Joey, it's awfully important for me to have your answers, and please be careful. I raised my dog from a six-weeks-old pup.

Yours with hopes,
Lee Langston

*P.S. If you get a chance to pen the dog up, please hold
him till I can get there. You will be rewarded, or anybody
else that does it.*

Three uneventful days passed, but they were meaningful
days to Lee, since they carried mounting suspense. He wondered, with dwindling hope, if Joey Barnes would answer his
letter, and if Joey's reply would bring any worth-while news.
Finally, the answer came, written in a scrawly hand on ruled
tablet paper:

Dear Lee:

*Your letter came. I am well an' I hope you are to.
About your dog or who's ever it is, yes the dog was
marked the way you said. What I could see of him was,
I mean. He was so mudy and full of burs I don't want
to be to sure for I don't wan't to misslead you.*

*It was funny about the gobler and how that dog bel-
lowed an took off like a scalded cat. I bet he was turkey-
whupped back when he was a pup. I can't say I saw the
whites of his eyes, but I did see a tucked tail an it seamed
like he was in such a hurry his hind end was trying to get
in ahead of his front end, ha. ha.*

*The dog's eyes was bloodshot so I can't say they looked
kind. At least they dident look mean. The chances are I
won't get a chance to pen him up an' get your reward.*

*I hope you find your dog. I had a pup once, a black-
antan hound that had such a good nose, but he got
maddog bit an we had to kill him. Pa did I mean, account of the rabbis.*

*If you ever get up thisaway look me up an we will set
out some hooks for catfish. The river is low now an they
are bitin' good. I got one last night that wayed 8teen*

*pounds after I had drug him up from the bottom to old
man Huckaby's store. It was a yellow cat an they are the
best kind to eat. I caught him on a son pearch the size
of your hand. The size of my hand I mean, for I don't
know how big your hand is, ha. ha.*

yrs.
Joey Barnes

*ps. Yes I could see the dog's hair was curly. There is a
maddog scare on now.*

The letter from Joey Barnes did little to ease Lee's suspense.
There was, however, one good feature of it: nothing in the
letter destroyed Lee's hope.

Having read Joey's letter, Mrs. Langston laughed. "Each to
his own interest," she said. "Your new friend seems to like
catfishing. And by the way, how does he know a 'son' perch
from a 'daughter' perch?"

Lee grinned briefly, studying the letter for some shred of
hope he may have overlooked in the first reading. "Too bad
about him losin' his hound pup," he said slowly.

"Yes, and he means 'rabies' instead of 'rabbis.' There's a
very big difference." Then she saw how worried Lee's face had
grown. "Now, don't start foreseeing the worst. About the
mad-dog scare, I mean. It won't help—"

"You know how most people are about a strange dog when
somebody yells, 'Mad dog!' " Lee pointed out. "They grab
guns and start shootin'."

"People these days wouldn't shoot a dog like Sad unless
he showed signs of hydrophobia. He's too pretty a dog. If he
foamed at the mouth or went about snapping at things, that
would be different."

Lee had turned as she was talking and was heading outside.

She knew why he had left the room. There was a double fear now burdening him. If Sad escaped being shot by some hysterical citizen, he was still in danger of suffering slower, more dreadful death from the bite of an infected dog or fox. With a boy's weakness for vivid imagination, Lee visualized the Llewellyn caught by the dread disease, changed from a hungry, hobo dog into a public menace with every man's hand against him.

He went outdoors, his eyes burning and blinking against the ache of dammed-up tears. He walked fast toward the empty pen, moving fast, as if with purpose, yet his only purpose was to be alone. He had once seen a mad dog, a shaggy, yellow stranger from no one knew where, had seen him moving, foam-mouthed, at a fast, automatonlike trot along a field road, snapping aimlessly at weeds and sprouts. From the tree he had climbed, Lee had watched his father and two other men go with their guns to kill the poor thing, which was driven and helpless in the grip of the mysterious infection.

Lee still remembered clearly the three men running across the pasture to head off the dog. They had run in a crouch, saying nothing, shotguns ready save for the cocking and shouldering. Lee was ten years old at the time, but he still remembered the cold, shivery feeling that had raced up and down him as he sat in the crotch of the persimmon tree and watched the men gain on the shaggy dog, which continued to travel at the same gait, as if propelled by some strange compulsion of unvarying force.

At a bend in the dirt road, which brought the dog into full view, the growth having been cleared there, the men stopped and brought their guns up. Lee thought his dad's gun had fired first, but he could not be sure. The three reports had sounded almost as one, and the dog had fallen forward, crumpling oddly, and for a swift second had contorted as if to snap at the searing pain that had struck him. Then he had rolled over and lain very still.

Lee stood at the pen gate, remembering that day and tying it up with the present. Foolish, of course, but suspense and love and fear can fuse together and twist the mind into silly exaggerations. Lee could plainly see Black Saddle, red-eyed and insane with fever, trotting at a steady gait along a field road, and he could see men with shotguns running across open land to head off the big, strange black-and-white setter.

He bit his lip and choked back the hot, swollen feeling in his throat. Then he wheeled away from the pen and went aimlessly, stumbling now and then, for where he stepped was of no matter.

When he stopped, he was under the shed where the tractor was kept, so he busied himself desperately with prying blocks of mud from the deep ridges of the right rear tire.

Two mornings later there was another account of the shaggy wanderer. A fifteen-year-old farm boy near Three Points, had succeeded in lassoing the dog and had tied him up for the night. Waking up deep in that night, the boy, proud of his new acquisition, had slipped out to check on him. He had found only the frazzled end of the rope remaining. The setter had gnawed loose and gone!

"And several miles south of Three Points," the announcer continued, "one of our listeners fed just such a dog this morning. He was wearing a piece of rope, with the frazzled end about his neck, or maybe tied to his collar. He was dripping wet and muddy. Our informant was sure that he had just swum the Hatchie River." The announcer paused for a moment, then added, "One thing is certain, neighbors: the dog keeps on going in the same direction. He must have a built-in compass!"

Four more days passed, bringing no more news of the hobo setter. Lee kept his radio tuned to that station when he was at home; and while he was at work Mrs. Langston listened.

"I hope this is a continued story," Mrs. Langston said. "I don't want it to end like this."

"Somebody caught him," Lee reasoned. "Or killed him. I still think it was Sad. I *know* it was!"

"No, you don't," Mr. Langston put in. "You just want to think it was."

Lee knew that his father was trying hard to prepare him for the worst, in case it came. That was part of a father's job. Mothers take the bright view, but fathers must be shock absorbers for their sons and daughters, presenting both sides of matters.

Deep in the night of the fourth day, Lee dreamed that he heard Sad barking. It was a vivid dream. The barks came faintly at first, then gradually in greater volume.

Still asleep, or in the vague state that lies between waking and sleeping, Lee called, "*Sad!*" But his voice came out in a labored whisper, as in a nightmare. The dog was barking more loudly now, almost deafeningly—

Mrs. Langston's voice broke through: "*Lee!* Come downstairs, Lee!"

He rolled from his bed. The room was dark. He stood groggily, trying to wake up enough to be sure that he was not dreaming. Yes, a dog *was* barking. His voice was rough and hoarse—

Lee ran for the gaunt dog

But Lee knew that Sad was back home again! He ran for the door.

Mr. Langston was on the back porch, the yardlight on. Lee burst through the screen door, his mother right behind him.

The dog in the back yard was scarcely more than an apparition. Only a few of his barks came through, most of his efforts ending in squeaks and wheezes. The animal was standing in the light from the back porch bulb, a gaunt, red-eyed, tottery beast caked with mud, his long hair matted and stained. His ears, once silken and curly, hung heavy now, ripped and slashed. A short length of frazzled rope swung from his neck.

With a choking sob of gladness, Lee ran for the gaunt creature. He fell on his knees, arms around the dog. The setter's rough, dry tongue was harsh against the boy's face, and the hair along the dog's neck was coarse and hard.

Lee's father and mother turned and went quietly back into the house.

It was a long time of welcoming, for Sad had worked hard for it and Lee had waited long for it. When it was over, Lee led the way to the pen, the bony wanderer moving stiffly alongside him. Then Lee brought food and water and stood, watching, while Sad gulped the meal, grunting and whining in gratitude.

When the dog had finished, Lee removed the collar and Sad stretched out in the cool safety of his pen. Back at the house, Lee discovered that Sad's second name had been "Wingo," and that his second owner had been a J. T. Hastings, of Wentworth.

"That's about forty miles north of Lindenwood," Mr. Langston said. "Sad traveled a pretty straight line, and well over a hundred miles."

"What I want to know," Lee said, "is where Mr. J. T. Hastings got this Wingo."

"We'll find out. As soon as it's polite. I'll get in touch with the sheriff. It's just about two-thirty now."

"And I'll write the announcer on that farm program tomorrow," Lee promised. "He'll be glad."

"You should write to Joey Barnes, too," Mrs. Langston reminded him. "Maybe you'll want to go up there and set out catfish hooks with him some time."

"I'll write and tell him," Lee promised, "but there won't be any time for me to go catfishing with Joey Barnes. I've got to get Sad back in shape before the bird season opens."

By shortly after eight the next morning, the wheels of justice had started turning. Sheriff Taylor had Mr. J. T. Hastings on the phone.

In the sheriff's office with his father, Lee could hear both ends of the conversation. Mr. Hastings was plainly excited by the call. He spoke loudly and with feeling.

"Yes, sir, Wingo was my dog," the man admitted. "I let him out for exercise when I thought he was used to his new home, and he took off." Further questions brought further details: Mr. Hastings had bought the dog from a man in Memphis, who had papers showing that it was a Tomlin setter. "I paid him a hundred and twenty-five dollars with a check made out to Cash," Mr. Hastings recalled. "He wanted it like that." Then, aware that he was in trouble, Mr. Hastings looked up the canceled check and reported that it had been endorsed by a Dr. Eddley, of Memphis.

"That Guy Tomlin works for him!" Lee exclaimed.

Immediately after talking with Mr. Hastings, the sheriff called Dr. Eddley. "Yes, I remember that check," he admitted. "Guy Tomlin owed me some money, and I took the check. No, I didn't ask him to endorse it, since it was to Cash. Of course, I endorsed it for deposit, as I do all checks I receive."

Confronted with such evidence, Guy Tomlin confessed his guilt, but he stoutly insisted that it was his own dog he had sold. But the court took a rather solemn view of the matter, for he had not only "broken and entered," but he had also transported stolen property across a state line and had sold it. His interest in dogs would not be of importance for the next thirty months.

Sad improved fast as the summer ran out. He was perfectly contented to remain in his pen, sleeping much of the time, resting luxuriously after his grueling time of travel and hunger and danger.

Soon after Lee had bathed and brushed the setter's coat, it began to shine and curl again. By late September, Sad had regained the weight he had lost, also the liveliness. On cool mornings he barked pleadingly when Lee went out to feed him, and he leaped and whirled about the boy, crouching and thrashing his tail. He could not have said more plainly with words, "Let's go! Let's take a hunt over the sedge hills and down through the hollows. Get your gun. I'll find birds for you. Come, boy!"

It was a slow time for Lee, waiting for the season to come again. October dragged by. The hours at school were far too long. The late afternoons and Saturdays in the dry, hot cotton-field moved on snail feet.

In late October the weather was cool, on the edge of frost. The hickory leaves were bright gold along the ridges, and sweet-gum trees were masses of crimson against the shades of buff and tan and russet of the less dramatic foliage. Sumacs were bright red, and the scattered pines, as if in calm contempt of the season's changes, stood contented in their constant dark green.

When at last the season opened, Lee and his father found Sad much steadier than before. He was grown now, settling down. He fell on point surely, with less winding and trailing, and he held his points rock-steady, not leaping in now to flush birds. He had settled down to finding singles. No longer did he run and bark after birds. One late afternoon, after losing sight of Sad in thick bushes, Lee and his father found him lying down, belly to ground, tail straight out, the tip curved a little upward.

"He's on point," Mr. Langston said. "Got tired of standing up, so he just settled down to wait. Walk in ahead of him."

Lee flushed the single, which streaked up and disappeared into the bushes before he could shoot.

"He's held that bird a half hour, at least!" the boy marveled. "We'd better rename him. How 'bout 'Rock of Gibraltar'?"

Sad retrieved now with sureness and style, apparently remembering what Embry had taught him last season. He watched for a bird to fall at gunshot, then streaked after it. Usually making a quick find, he picked up the limp quail and came trotting, highheaded, holding his prize by a wing or loosely by body, never crushing it. As he had been taught, he always brought the bird to Lee. Deciding who had dropped the bird was up to the hunters, of course, for Sad was not a bookkeeper.

Lee's shooting had improved. He could now pick out a bird on the covey rise and drop it neatly three out of five shots.

The wild nervousness he had felt last season, with the roar of a rising covey, had not left him, but he could control it better.

"Will I ever get over feelin' that my heart's about to fly out of my body when a covey flares up?" Lee asked his father.

"I reckon not. I'm that way, too. There's something about those wonderful little wings that makes a fellow's blood run faster. To be honest, I hope you never get over it—and I don't, either. It's a real part of bird hunting."

Lee thought about what his father had said. It seemed that a man who had hunted for years would be hardened to the thrill of whirring wings. Maybe that was the very heart of bird hunting, the thing that kept some men at it until they were too feeble to walk after dogs. It was a kind of hunting geared to all ages from boyhood on through. And there were good reasons, he decided:

A dog is on point, not seeing the birds but knowing by the intensity of the odor that if he takes one more step ahead he may be guilty of the grave error of flushing. The hunter, sure of his dog, knowing the birds are there, yet not wanting to see them, not even wanting to know how they will veer on the rise, for this is the exciting uncertainty of it, moves in ahead of the stone-still dog. He knows that out of this tense tableau, out of the blending growth and silence and motionlessness and invisibility there will suddenly be an airful of swift wings and plump bodies, dark little masses of speed and purpose, transforming silence and nothingness into scattering sight and sound, each to seek its own covert—if spared—until they can gather again in the twilight of that day. The more Lee thought about it, the more he began to recognize the fascinations of bird-hunting. It held man-and-dog certainty and uncertainty, mystery, action, life-and-death, grace, cruelty, speed, sound and that was enough for any kind of hunting to hold!

When the season was yet young, Embry came out on a Saturday with two borrowed pointers. "He's got to learn to hunt with other dogs," he said. "He's got to learn how to 'back' any dog that drops on point in sight of him."

"You're mighty nice to take up time with Sad," Lee told him.

"Well, he's a fine dog, an' I guess he's the last Tomlin I'll have a chance to try my hand on." Then he said to Mr. Langston, more than to Lee, "If it's a boy, we'll name him after Mary Lou's gran'pa."

"Well, now!" Mr. Langston exclaimed. "I'm so proud to hear that. It'll be a big help."

"We're mighty excited about it, Mary Lou an' me," Embry said. "You tell Mrs. Langston."

"She'll be plumb happy to hear it, I tell you!"

Winter came. Sad was averaging three days a week in the field, never tiring. Mr. Langston and Mr. Webb hunted together while Lee was at school. Mr. Langston and Embry and Lee, with Sad and borrowed dogs, hunted on some Saturdays. On others, Lee and Embry roamed the ridge to the west in dry weather, and on damp days they worked the edge of the creek bottom.

Whenever Embry could leave work early enough in the afternoon, he came to the Langston place. Sad, it seemed, had grown into an obsession with him. He worked endlessly, and at every opportunity, to sharpen the dog's style.

"The little bitty things you bother about," Lee said one afternoon, curiosity aroused, "won't make any difference in everyday huntin', will they?"

"Not a bit," Embry agreed. "But, Lee, I've got somethin' on my mind besides everyday huntin'."

"You left me way behind," Lee told him. "Catch me up."

"I want to take Sad to the Great Southern in February. They judge the fine points there."

Lee's eyes widened. "The Great Southern? After the way he disgraced us all in the puppy trials last year?"

"That was last year. Sad's past all that. Look, Lee, I want to do this for several reasons: for *you*, for *me* an' for *Sad*. The middle reason is the biggest one, I'll admit. If I could take Sad to the Great Southern an' make a good showin', ol' Mr. Tomlin would think a lot more of me. You'd trust me to . . ."

"Sure, I'd trust you!" Lee broke in happily. "And, man, if you could win there—"

"Don't count on that," Embry warned, to hold down false hopes. "He'll be up against some fine dogs, the best in the South—also points north, east and west! But if he could just make a good showin'."

"He will," Lee said eagerly. "I know he will. Let's talk to Dad about it."

Again Mr. Tomlin had Christmas dinner with the Langstons. During the meal Lee said, "We're thinkin' about puttin' Sad in the Great Southern Field Trials in February."

"That so?" The old man's eyes were alight. "Is he trained out of his puppy foolishness, you think?"

"Embry has worked mighty hard with him. Nobody else could do a better job of handlin' Sad at the Great Southern."

"*What?*" The old man sat back a little, his craggy face hard. "A Wales handlin' a Tomlin dog in the Great Southern?" It was rank heresy.

"But Embry's *good* with dogs," Lee declared.

Mr. Tomlin thought for a moment, his bushy brows busy. "It's your setter," he said finally, then drank hot coffee, making a sibilant sound.

January was cold and blustery, with little weather fit for hunting. February came in mild and pretty, but cold enough for a bird dog to work.

Embry took half of his year's vacation for the Great Southern. He left early one morning in late February, with Sad in a big crate in the bed of the pickup. In addition to the truck, Mr. Langston had supplied him with money for entry fee and expenses.

"I wouldn't take this," Embry said, flushing, "except that I've got some extra expenses headin' my way before long."

"Win one of the purses," Lee told him, "and you can pay this back and put the rest in your pocket." And, feeling right manly, "Dad and I have talked it over."

"Yes, *sir!*" Embry said with a grin.

For the next three days Lee was in school in name only. He went through the required motions from class to class, remaining out of trouble. He kept seeing Sad racing out with some pointer or setter—and men on horses—and truckloads of dogs that had been hunted to a fine edge by professionals who knew all the angles. Sad was in very fast company now.

On the second day of the trials, the Memphis paper to which the Langstons subscribed reported on the first day of competition:

> . . . and another Tomlin setter, called Black Saddle, is setting the pace in the Great Southern. Older men there are watching him and remembering his famous ancestors and

their great performances. It is too early to predict any kind of outcome, but Black Saddle has everything—

It was a great night for Lee Langston. He lay wide awake during most of it. When he shut his eyes, he saw Sad flowing along a ridge or stiff on point or trotting stiff-legged down the quail-fragrant wind—

The next day's paper brought news that another dog, a pointer, was pushing Sad hard:

Handled by Mr. Flem Branch, a big 'rip-rap' pointer named Big Jim is turning in fine performances in all departments. It will be great competition if these two dogs meet in the finals.

"Jim!" Lee said excitedly. "That's the dog that jumped on Sad the first day he hunted."

"He didn't lick Sad then," Mr. Langston said calmly, holding back his excitement. "Maybe he won't this time."

On the night of the final day, Lee dialed until he found a broadcast of the Great Southern outcome: "And the Tomlin won," the announcer was saying dramatically. "He swamped the 'rip-rap' in both finds and form. As in the old days, a big black-and-white setter of the Tomlin line was unbeatable. Missing, though, was the tall, red-haired dean of trainers, Mr. Luke Tomlin—although he had a fine replacement in young Embry Wales, grandson-in-law of the man whose spirit as a dedicated bird-dog man will always go where there's a Tomlin setter, for he built a lot of himself into that famous line—"

Lee was numb with joy. He stood there, staring at the radio. He was breathing fast through dry, parted lips. "*EEEEYEEEOOOWWW!*" he yelled, putting everything into it. Words were so inadequate right then. All the pent-up hopes that had made suspense so sharp were in the cry. "Sad won!" he yelled, wheeling to go downstairs.

"He won!" Mrs. Langston almost screamed from the foot of the steps. "Our dog won!"

"You had the same broadcast on," Lee said breathlessly, tumbling down to meet her; and when he reached his mother, he did a strange thing for Lee Langston. He threw his arms about her and hugged her so hard she struggled for freedom.

"Goodness!" she gasped. "You'll still need your poor mother, even if Sad did win!" And she kissed him on the cheek . . . a rare thing for her to do, Lee being the kind of boy he had been.

"You all sound surprised," Mr. Langston said as he came out into the hall.

"Smarty!" Mrs. Langston said shrilly. "You almost turned handsprings when the word came. Come, let's get to town and tell Mary Lou. She hasn't heard yet, maybe."

"Don't you reckon Embry has called her?" Mr. Langston asked.

"Maybe he hasn't. Anyway, this is a time to share such wonderful news! Let's go."

It was a fast ride to town, but to Lee it seemed slow. Halfway there, Mrs. Langston said to him, "Don't lean so far ahead. You won't beat us there."

Mary Lou was not at the little apartment over the dime store. "She's down at the hospital," a neighbor woman told the Langstons. "Mary Lou had a little boy today."

"A boy!" Mrs. Langston cried. "For heaven's sake! Why didn't somebody call me? Come on, you two."

At the hospital they found Mary Lou's room, and there

they found a very happy young mother. "Embry called just a little while ago," she told them. "He's on his way home right now. Lord, it's wonderful to have two winners at the same time, Embry and little Luke."

"Named him for his great-gran'daddy, huh?" Mr. Langston asked.

"What'd you expect?" a rough voice asked.

They turned toward the door and saw old Luke Tomlin standing there. His white hair was tousled, his bushy brows twitching busily. "That Embry did a fine job," he said. "I always knew that boy had good stuff in him, an' now he's proved it!"

"Grandpa's been here all day," Mary Lou said. "He's as proud as I am."

"Who wouldn't be proud of a day like this?" the old man asked as he contentedly tamped rough-cut into his battered pipe. Then, in a voice soft with good anticipation, "It'll be like a long time ago, havin' a little fellow runnin' about the old Tomlin place out there!"

"Bless you!" Mrs. Langston said happily. "In fact, bless everybody!"